ISBN 978-1-9998168-0-3

Raebird
Books

June 2019
raebirdbooks.com

For

My Mother, Ishbel Karam
and for Kerry, Peter and Chris

Dedicated to

My Grandmother, Marion Rae
and My Father, Dr Khalid Karam

CONTENTS

CHAPTER ONE

"Do you know why you're here?"

The question could be considered on so many levels. Robbie looked at the edge of the desk where the veneer was lifting off the cheap chipboard core. He looked at the sight test poster – going straight for the bottom, most challenging, line of letters. He looked anywhere but at Dr Hawkins. The silence ticked on until he felt himself shrug reluctantly. Unable to think of sentences, or even words, to express his feelings, he just focused on the letters... X, U, R, J, G, Y, M.

"It's hard to explain, maybe? Your mother is worried about you and we just want to make sure that you know that you can talk if you need to. These things can't be forced. We're not annoyed with you."

More silence. Robbie wondered how much he weighed and what blood pressure really was.

"I don't know what I feel or what to say. Maybe I don't feel anything much. Sometimes I try to think about what I'm thinking and I can't even do that," he said eventually.

"I'll be honest with you," the doctor confided, "I feel that you may be a little depressed and, given the circumstances, this is quite natural. Depression is an illness suffered by huge numbers of people and there are different ways we can help you get back to feeling your old self."

Robbie shrugged again. He wasn't old, but he wasn't himself. Something about him felt lost and distracted and sad, it wouldn't stop and most of the time he just wanted to be by himself. He no longer felt like the mischievous young man who'd mooched around Harrow town centre with his mates, daring each other to get into varying degrees of trouble. Although that wasn't a bad thing as, really, he'd been a nuisance, he realised now. He wanted something better but, annoyingly, he couldn't even attempt to put his feelings into words. All Robbie knew was that there must be more to life than this.

The tick of the clock bounced around between the polystyrene ceiling tiles and the linoleum flooring. There was nothing natural in this room, it seemed, except his response to crisis. Normal. Understandable. But Robbie had become a stranger to himself. He was a shell, he felt empty and hollow.

The doctor could sense the boy's frustration and the anxiety that further probing would only exacerbate. Few people were as reluctant as Robbie to talk about themselves and their problems. Another, less patient, patient would readily drop their year-old magazine and recite a list of ailments.

"I don't want to push you into talking when you can't find the words," Dr Hawkins announced, shifting forward on his seat. "I certainly don't want you to say something just because you think it's what I want to hear. Things will get better, in time, but I want to meet with you again soon. I've given your mother a leaflet, you can read it if you feel like it." The doctor stood up, his trousers hiding the bright red socks that Robbie had settled his gaze on. Blinking, Robbie looked directly at the doctor for the first time.

"Can I go now?"

The doctor smiled without showing his teeth and nodded.

Robbie's mother, Mrs Alderson, had been watching a mauve betta fish in a tank near the reception desk. She knew her son's every sigh. She knew the difference between his walk and shuffle and strut; able to tell his mood without even looking. Despite this, these last few weeks had been difficult because these deciphering skills had rarely been needed. Robbie was always in the same fog and she no longer felt the need to keep one step ahead of his antics. She could hear the dragging of his feet as he made his way past the desk of the austere receptionist. Robbie just wanted to leave, she instantly concluded, he did not want – or need – further interrogation. Mrs Alderson also smiled without showing her teeth and nodded. As she squashed the leaflet into her jacket pocket and thanked the staff, Robbie sauntered to the door and wished he was invisible. His face didn't look happy or sad, it just looked blank; like he was staring at a never-ending computer game that someone else was playing.

Outside the bracing wind quickly undid the soporific effects of the ticking clocks and floating fish inside the surgery. Robbie let the salty air hit his face like a slap to the panic-stricken. He could hear his heart beat around his temple, inside his hood.

"Alright love?" his mother said. It was not really a question and it didn't require a response. None was given.

Robbie lifted his focus from the road onto the fields around them. It was a far cry from Harrow centre; from the kebab shops and cafes and charity collectors patrolling the grubby streets. Concrete, metal and glass were replaced by every conceivable permutation of brown – from washed out beige to deep, damp muddy russet. Busy-ness and businesses had been replaced with nothingness and quiet. The bleak, never-ending barbed wire fences and dry-stone walls were an unsatisfactory substitute for the pedestrian precinct, shopping centre and cinema complex. This was Unst, Britain's most northerly tip, one of the islands in Shetland. This was the edge of Robbie's world.

Four months ago, Robbie's mother, Ruth, had been left enough money to relocate and start a whole new venture. With house prices around London soaring, and Robbie finding it harder to balance his stubborn independence with his need to be accepted by his peers, Ruth decided her money, and patience, would go further somewhere rural. Unst, with

3

its gentle pace and community values, had appealed to Ruth immediately. She felt that what the island lacked in entertainment and amenities it more than made up for in spiritual, educational and personal opportunities. Ruth was a brave woman who knew that the move would not be popular with her son, but she was the adult. Given the span of his lifetime, she hoped her son would forgive her for these few angry months in adolescence. She was looking at the bigger picture and she would not let Robbie dictate what was going to make the man of him.

Robbie had been so preoccupied and troubled by all his other feelings, he did not have the energy to be aggressive towards his mother at every given opportunity. And he knew that, ultimately, she had always wanted the best for him and she was also going through her own personal hell.

The walk home was verbally silent, but the noise of the wind would have made talking challenging anyway. With no trees and few buildings, Robbie wondered what made the wind whistle and rumble as it did. The sea was the new view. Where once he had looked to billboards and architectural lines for visual stimuli, here the waves and turbulent tides engaged him in a way nothing else could. The tempestuous nature of the water, its pounding and ferocious drive, seemed to present him with a scene comparable with his inner turmoil; it was the only thing which seemed to understand him.

Ruth was busy. Her way of coping with change, and the all-consuming job of ignoring her emotions, was to throw herself into her new Bed and Breakfast business. Key to this, and part of the reason for moving, was to meet people in the local area and, hopefully, make friends. Unst was like a big family. She knew instantly that she could be a 'somebody' here whereas, in Harrow, she might have always been a 'nobody'.

Unst had an ageing population of around 600 people. There had been a steady decline since the 1980s when it had housed an RAF base and an airport used by the oil industry. Ruth's older brother, Chris, had been stationed here before the decommissioning and had always recounted his deployment with affection. Even he admitted, however, that there was a period of adjustment and that the winters were exceptionally long and dark. Two shops and a bakery provided essentials; the supermarket was a five-hour round-trip away. The village halls and small leisure centre were the hub of social activity.

Most people visited Unst for peace and quiet, Robbie had deduced. However, he could also see that it was easier to find someone to talk, laugh and dance with on Unst than in any big city. Everyone was a friend by virtue of the fact they relied on each other, and waving at all passers-by seemed mandatory.

The fresh air and wide expanse of landscape that filled the view to the very horizon replenished the spirit with something invigorating and pure through the day. Evenings could then be filled with camaraderie and activity; music nights, community suppers and historic talks.

There were hardly any pavements and some streets were barely wide enough for a single tractor. The only graffiti Robbie had seen on the whole island was where someone (probably a visitor) had written 'wind' between the words on the square 'Passing Place' sign. Seeing it was the only time Robbie could remember smiling since he'd arrived. No-one saw him.

Robbie and his mother walked near the verge of the tarmac, trying to stay between the traffic (of which there was almost none) and the ditch. The roadside ditches held a growing fascination to Robbie because they were a strange mix of wild plants and empty beer cans. As spring progressed, the flowers grew ever more vivid, but the litter mysteriously disappeared. It later transpired that locals cleaned up the ditches before the height of the tourist season. Excitingly today, in a puddle of ditch water, Robbie spotted a blubbery mass of frogspawn. He stopped. Ruth

5

stopped too and watched her son lower himself nearer. He broke off a dried hogweed stem and poked the eggs gently.

"Come back and collect some of them later," Robbie's mother said, knowing what he was thinking. "Don't damage them, we'll find a container to keep them in."

Robbie pushed his nippy fingers deep into his pockets. His left hand curled around a strange pebble he'd found on his first visit to the beach near the Post Office. They were nearly home, nearly back to the Bed and Breakfast where Ruth had yet more guest laundry to do and Robbie's only designated duty for the evening was to set the table. His mother insisted they ate dinner together every day and, as she could be a formidable force, he felt it was in his best interests not to argue.

Unst was a safe and traditional haven in a world that couldn't keep pace with itself anymore. Many families did not lock their houses or cars. Bikes were left at the roadside, ready to be collected after hillside walks and Ruth could leave Robbie alone to discover himself, unlike in the city. But despite all this new freedom, Robbie was usually to be found in the isolated sanctuary of his bedroom on his portal to Cyber Space. Things would change, but it would take time. Thankfully, Unst had time and so did Robbie.

This afternoon was already different. As more of Ruth's bedsheets reached the dizzy crescendo of the spin cycle, Robbie and a plastic bucket were making their way back to the frogspawn.

CHAPTER TWO

Robbie had been born and brought up around Harrow, a borough in North West London. The community was very mixed; different nationalities, languages, food and ages ensured a diverse and rich cultural experience. Of course, Robbie wasn't aware that this was 'diversity'; he didn't know any different, it was just home.

The town centre had seen changes, even during Robbie's life. He had often hung out at the new shopping centre with his friends, eating nutritionally dubious food and laughing at passers-by. When he was eventually allowed a skateboard, he spent hours in the tiled underpass between the cinema and the unfinished block of flats.

Robbie's favourite place was Harrow Recreation Ground, a Victorian park situated next to a large cemetery. There was always something to watch in this open space – kite flyers, cricketers in their white kit, joggers and football practice. The tennis and basketball courts were never empty. For Robbie, the park filled his senses. The sound of children's laughter, rummaging dogs and cricket balls being knocked interrupted the rustle of leaves and gentle bird song. In spring, huge cherry trees blossomed in pink, lining the path to the bowling green. Crisp white lines marked the pitches and couples sat, kissing, on the benches near the play park. The cool water of the drinking fountain always splashed onto the front of his t-shirt, a collection of nuts and seeds, cones and leaves, always found its way into his pocket. He remembered his parents bringing him here as a young child, playing Frisbee. He remembered the smell of damp soil and moss after it rained, of perfumed flowers and freshly cut grass. The park had been his special place.

The cemetery gate was always ajar, and Robbie had first explored it by himself (although it was the middle of the day, when it was bright and sunny). Graveyards held a fascination; they reminded him of his mortality at a time when he felt invincible; they humbled him as each person's life was reduced to a few dates and words; they saddened him when he saw engraved ages younger than his own, and families who had lost many. History was very much alive in the cemetery. Here Robbie could find mention of jobs, relationships, diseases, tragedies, achievements and love. He could also see signs of the contemporary world; graffiti, vandalism, littering, loitering, disrespect, delinquency. It was here Robbie had first tasted alcohol and here he had rejected his first offer of a cigarette. He was thankful that neither had enthralled him but, as he got older his need for peer acceptance would lure him into other kinds of shenanigans. Parental love was not enough to stop that.

Robbie's father had watched his son with a careful and protective eye since the very first moment he'd held him at Northwick Park Hospital. Ruth was the more pragmatic of the two parents. Nathan was more likely to relent to his son's requests, however questionable. He too had grown up around London, he knew city life was a harsh teacher and he wanted to give his son everything that he never had.

It was a Saturday evening seven months ago when the call came.

"Mrs Alderson? ... I'm afraid there's been an accident."

Nathan's car had been hit at a junction by a drunk driver trying to evade the police. Ruth and Robbie had rushed to the hospital, but his father was already unconscious. Most of what happened during the following two days was a blur, but Robbie could still close his eyes and smell his dad's room and hear the sound of the respirator. Out of view, Nathan was given the tests to determine his chances of recovery, but the news wasn't good. Robbie heard snatches of conversations and whisperings which were not meant for children's ears. Other patients in intensive care were cosseted by streams of relatives who wept and read and sometimes sang quietly in the public areas. Robbie didn't know whether or not he should cry. His mother was a very strong woman and kept trying to be optimistic, but the prognosis was not positive. Nathan lay still, his eyes unresponsive, his tickle-proof feet tucked in by his wife's pale hands. Robbie's father was all but gone; all that remained was the shell that had housed his memories, his consciousness, his laughter and his soul. Gone. Even though the machine ensured the colour still sat on his cheeks and his weak pulse throbbed in his neck, Nathan – the husband, the joker, the friend and father – was gone. The doctors declared him brain dead on Monday after Robbie had had a very dry Ploughman's sandwich. It was strange the things Robbie could remember.

He was told Nathan had died in Ruth's arms and did not suffer. Robbie had said goodbye earlier in the day and was at home with Ruth's mother who had come over from Northern Ireland.

The next two weeks were fuzzy in Robbie's mind. He began to believe that funerals were invented to keep people busy and together at a time when they would ordinarily fall apart. He slept a lot, ate little and stared at the television passively. He had no father. He had no father.

Very quickly – too quickly for Robbie, if he was honest – Ruth decided they had to leave London and start again somewhere new, somewhere safe.

"I know I should have involved you more in this decision, son," she had said with genuine acknowledgement, "but I can't stay here. I can't be the best mother for you unless we make changes. You have to trust me."

Ruth told Robbie that she had bought a Bed and Breakfast business on Unst and that they would be moving. She thought she was doing the right thing, maybe it was the only course of action she could cope with. Unfortunately, it also meant that Robbie had not only lost his dad, but also faced losing his unbefitting friends, skating in the underpass, throwing popcorn at the back of the cinema and the fall of the pink cherry blossom. Robbie began to lose himself in the haze.

With his mother's aspidistra wedged between his knees, Robbie had reluctantly settled in the passenger seat for the long drive to Aberdeen. It was a crisp morning and the road glistened until dawn broke somewhere just north of Cambridge. Ruth played gentle funky jazz and slurped on a travel mug of pungent black coffee to help her stay awake. The soft vibration and light rhythm helpfully coaxed Robbie to sleep, allowing the journey to pass far quicker than it did for Ruth. Her own personal drive kept her satisfied at the wheel, only taking rest breaks when they were crucial. Hours and hours passed.

Aberdeen appeared to be the greyest, dullest, hardest place that Robbie had ever come across. Thick, misty clouds hung low over the tallest buildings and he could almost taste the dampness in the air. Granite block-work facades were only softened by the curves and colours of umbrellas and anoraks. The wipers waved furiously as Ruth's Ford Escort crawled, as if exhausted, to the port. Despite the eleven hour drive, Shetland was still a fourteen hour ferry ride away.

This part of the journey, under more cheerful circumstances, would have been novel and exciting. Robbie had never been on a boat of this size and his imagination began to stir for the first time in weeks.

The port smelled of fish, sea and grease. Gulls looped over the vessels moored nearby. Everyone looked busy and preoccupied. A couple in bright cagoules carefully studied a map while their children ran rings around them.

On board the ceilings were lower than Robbie had expected. Long, straight, carpeted corridors lead down the length of the boat. Cabin 108 was clean and utilitarian. It contained two beds, one above the other, a small shower room and rectangular window. The Ford was somewhere in the belly of the hull, waiting to be transported to a new habitat. After a deep bellow from the funnels, the boat moved gently from its moorings, from the city, from civilisation, and into the choppy, unforgiving waters of the North Sea.

Fourteen hours later, after a dark, hot and restless night, Robbie and his mother stood looking across to the main town on the islands; Lerwick.

Unst was still two ferries away. Lying between was the island of Yell, where a seventeen-mile ribbon of tarmac spread across a bleak expanse of moor. Seeing nothing but sheep and a few scattered buildings, Robbie thought it was ironic – the island of Yell didn't have much to shout about.

A close look would have revealed the freshwater pools, acidic and peat-stained, the mini islands of blaeberries surrounded by rich blankets of sphagnum moss and the myriad of birds and insects. In the eyes of the car passengers however, these blurred into a homogeneous brown streak.

The passenger ferries proved to be a highlight. Up in the lounge area Robbie blew on his hot chocolate and stared, mesmerised, at the turbid waters of the sound. The second ferry journey, taking people from Yell to Unst, was quicker – less than ten minutes. The strong inlet tides rocked the vessel rather dramatically and no-one aboard ventured out of their vehicles. When the ramp lowered, the cars were waved off by a rotund man in a fluorescent jacket and Robbie got his first real view of the island that was to become his home.

A huge board, painted by local children and reminiscent of the graffiti in the underpass, made an unexpectedly contemporary welcome sign. Below this, and rather bizarrely, there was a wooden rowing boat which had been converted into a giant xylophone. The road curved sharply upwards in the opposite direction and Ruth drove the last few miles to their new home.

The village of Baltasound was the biggest on the island. Houses of varying size, shape and age were sprinkled around the water's edge, facing different directions and made of different materials. Was this indicative of how individual the residents were? He noticed the red roof of the leisure centre immediately as they descended the final hill. Near to it stood the health centre, church and care home, village hall, shop and Post Office. And between them all there was space, grass (brown, not green) and stone.

The Bed and Breakfast was a large white house with a black slate roof and two tall chimney stacks. As the busy season was about to start, Ruth had decided that she and Robbie would move into a small annex flat attached to the main building, opening up more bedrooms for guests.

Robbie found his room. It looked the same as it did on the website, maybe bigger. He lay on the floor and stared out the window at the clouds which were moving at speed from one side of the wooden frame to the other. The view from his Harrow bedroom had been limited by the neighbours' house – he had seen mostly brick wall with a hint of door. He listened to his mother busying herself. His breathing slowed, his limbs fell limp. Maybe there would be no choice but to relax here and enjoy the slower pace. Maybe this venture would be more about a change of emphasis, a change of perspective. Robbie wondered if he could consider quietness as 'meditation', rather than 'boredom'; 'doing nothing' as 'thinking space' and 'loneliness' as 'becoming self-reliant'... He looked up at the ever-shifting clouds. Nothing stays the same, he thought.

CHAPTER THREE

The Bed and Breakfast interior consistently smelled of washing powder. Sometimes there were gentle undertones of paint and polish but, as his mother washed every pillow case, duvet cover and towel in preparation for her first visitors, it was the fragrance of lavender and camomile that would forever remind Robbie of this period of readjustment.

Robbie's room was larger than his old one in Harrow. It was still a non-descript magnolia shade which had fulfilled its 'quick sale' purpose, but was now too insipid and void of personality. Robbie intended to paint over it but he had not decided on a suitable colour – or colours – yet, but there was no point putting up posters or photographs until the decorating was complete. The plain expanse of paint had its uses; for endless hours Robbie would stare at it, imagining things past, things future and, most often, things in a fantasy world.

To an onlooker, these lost hours of near motionless inactivity may have appeared to be wasted time, wasted opportunity, but to Robbie they seemed vital. These were some of the few occasions he felt in control. They were the times when his brain was rewiring its pathways, creating understanding and acceptance of his new world. These moments allowed him to slowly come to terms with all that had brought him to now. But now, right now, the reality of breathing and living and loving and hurting was too difficult. His thought pendulum kept swinging between past, future and fantasy, but at least it was swinging.

Once in a while Robbie needed to surface from his magnolia cave. Like a blind mole breaking through the grass roots and into the sunlight, Robbie would stumble, bleary-eyed and hungry, through his new house. Today, with only gentle encouragement and mild bribery from Ruth, he decided to venture even further from the lair and go for a wander.

Before leaving the house, Robbie had categorised the day as 'grey'. The overcast sky hung thick and low but there was life and growth here, whereas in Harrow there would have been concrete and shadows. Robbie began walking in no particular direction. So much sky – no buildings limiting the view. So much colour – his initial assessment had to be re-evaluated. On distant hills the auburn heather decorated the moorland and beckoned to be explored. The fields in the middle distance were shades of mud and shoots. Lambs bleated into the wind.

From every direction Robbie could hear the shrill cries of the birds dancing and diving to impress their prospective mates. Although unknown to him, the tumbling lapwings, the curlews and oystercatchers displayed and defended their territories with flourish and drama. The behaviour of birds was to hold, for Robbie, an initial intrigue and then a fascination. As his understanding grew, his interest in observation (coupled with the distraction and focus it offered him) would become a very helpful meditation. City pigeons had not held any appeal but the wild birds of Unst had to fight a lot harder for their gains and they deserved some attention and appreciation.

Robbie found himself heading to the coast. Where this would have been a long-planned day trip or weekend visit when in London, here it was little more than a half hour stroll. The smell of soil was replaced with a salty breeze, and along the roadside broken bits of mussel shell and sea urchin littered the gravel. Gulls and crows had dropped these colourful pieces onto the tarmac, hoping to break the outer casings and reveal the tasty morsels inside. Roadkill often offered them an easier meal. Whenever Robbie came across some he would try to identify it – more often than not, it was the remains of a rabbit or a hedgehog.

The beach was mostly made of rounded, grey pebbles the size of baking potatoes. Nearer to the water's edge there was a strip of wet sand which widened as the tide retreated. Across the bay was a sister beach, empty save for some brightly coloured buoys and a small boat which had been pulled high onto the bank. There were lots of small croft houses on the gentle slope which reflected in the water – many were uninhabited. Robbie looked over to find the road that snaked between the cottages, his eyes followed it back to his side of the bay and he decided that, soon, he would take some sandwiches and explore further afield.

Shafts of sunlight pierced the billowing grey clouds. Beams of brightness hit the water and a few lucky spots of land. With an appropriate number of layers on, the weather was bearable and refreshing, as long as the rain held off and the wind was not bitter. Between the seaweed Robbie found a sheltered area on the beach and he lay down on his back.

He closed his eyes. Realising he was tense, he took deep breaths and let his shoulders drop. His clenched fists opened and allowed his fingers to feel the worn sandstone under him. There was nothing to fear. The sounds of nature captured his attention as his breathing levelled and tension eased. The regular lapping of the water onto the sand, the short, sharp whistles of passing sandpipers, even the gentle buzzing of insects consumed him. For a few short minutes Robbie was in the present. Now.

Unsure of whether or not he had dozed off, or how long he had been on the stones, Robbie sat up feeling refreshed and more uplifted than he had in a long time. He noticed that the receding tide had revealed more shells, colourful flotsam and jetsam and glistening shingle. He wandered down the wet sand picking up rounded bits of glass and other random treasures. Soon, his jacket pockets were full of all manner of items and Robbie felt his beachcombing had come to an end for the day. The sun was lowering and the remains of the light was tinted with an orange glow. He found his mobile phone and, although there was usually no signal in this remote part of Scotland, he used it to take a few photographs of the sunset. In London, his mother would have worried about him and his whereabouts, but here, with no crime and no temptation, he felt sure she was more worried about how best to iron large cotton sheets.

Just as Robbie was daring himself to go home through the sheep field, he saw something moving in his peripheral vision. As he neared the source of the flapping he could see that an injured bird lay nestled between two larger rocks at the roadside. Afraid that the unfortunate creature had been hit by a passing car, Robbie stared at it and wondered if it could bite or stab him. The calm, still feeling of the beach was shattered by the laboured cries of the bird as Robbie approached – was he just upsetting it further in its final moments? Robbie worried that he might need to somehow 'put it out of its misery'. Even if he knew exactly what this would entail, he did not think he would be capable of doing it. This was, after all, a creature, albeit a rather unfamiliar one.

After some minutes the bird was too exhausted to maintain its attempts at protesting and resumed its position of limp stillness. Only one of its wings had moved, Robbie had noted. It was prudent to assume the other one was broken – damaged at the very least. This bird was going to die here unless Robbie did something and, even then, it might not make it, certainly not without suitable food and water. Robbie did not even know what type of bird it was. The 'black and white and orange' type – was that enough to Google?

Having been told numerous times, by countless people, Robbie was inclined to believe that he did indeed over-think things. His levels of analysis were rarely warranted. There was probably a hundred ways to pick up a bird. Some were intuitively wrong – only birds that had been shot were ever shown hanging by the tail. It seemed right to cup the middle of the frightened creature, with its wings closed. Robbie decided to go with this as it also seemed to keep danger areas (beak, claws and both messy ends) as far from his hands as possible.

Slowly Robbie moved closer and leaned over the bird with his arms outstretched. He opened his hands and separated them just enough to surround the warm, feathery body. He held the bird for a few seconds, hoping it would feel secure and allow Robbie to pick it up without struggle. But as he gently lifted his fingers he could sense the bird was going to resist and he tightened his grip firmly but with measured pressure. Both wings were neatly folded under his palms and, gradually, the bird's feet appeared below it. Robbie lifted it upwards and tried to tuck it inside his padded jacket. With a little protest, but not much choice in the matter, the bird allowed Robbie to position it safely. He folded his arms over and around the quilted bulge and walked briskly along the road.

As he headed for home, Robbie started to think about the bird and how he could help it. He was wondering what his mother would say about it and how he didn't even know what it would eat. Often, in times of difficulty, Robbie found that it was hard to think of anything outside his own head. He would forget things around him, like his mum's birthday, and he felt that he sometimes appeared rude and cut off. Most questions he was asked seemed undeserving of an answer. Most people seemed to be annoying him deliberately. He usually wished he could be left alone (even though this sometimes made him terrified and desperate for reassurance and company). But today he thought he would welcome any advice and help without eyeball rolling or groaning.

As he neared the house, Robbie headed for the shed which he knew contained several large, empty cardboard boxes. Tightening his hold with one hand, he used the other to open the door and remove a sturdy box from the pile. With slow and deliberate movements Robbie unzipped his jacket and freed the bird from its warm compartment. He placed it gently into the very bottom of the box and closed the lid. He could hear it flapping and scratching but, a few seconds later, it settled again. Robbie used an old screwdriver to make a couple of air holes in the top of the box and decided to put a few shells and pebbles from his collection into the bird's new home. He hoped the smell of familiar objects would reassure it. Using this opportunity to look again at the feathers, markings and plumage, Robbie recognised that he had seen this type of bird before. It was larger than a pigeon, with a black and white body and head, a long straight orange beak and long pink legs. Robbie watched to see if the bird was still alive, then he picked up the box and walked carefully towards the house.

CHAPTER FOUR

"Whatever that is," Ruth said "you need to get it out of here because we have our first visitors."

Robbie knew this was an important day for his mother so he immediately backed out, put the box down carefully in the porch and took off his muddy boots and jacket.

"Mum, I've found a bird and it's injured. It's in that box. I don't really know what to do. I don't even know what to feed it."

Ruth looked around at her son. His eyes showed a significant level of concern – something she had not seen in him for a long time. She shifted her gaze and stared into the middle distance, her brow furrowed, her lips pursed.

"I have no idea what to do but I was speaking to our guest and he seems to know a lot about local nature so maybe I could introduce you."

Mr Hughson was a hefty man. He wore sand coloured corduroy trousers and a knitted sweater full of pattern. His clean leather walking boots had been well used; Mr Hughson was more energetic than his rested posture seemed to indicate. His legs were outstretched and crossed at the ankles, and his balding head was covered with a cap, the words 'Fife Raptor Group' embroidered on its front. Robbie had no idea what a 'raptor' was.

"Mr Hughson, your evening meal will be ready in about 20 minutes," Ruth confirmed.

"Please call me Charlie," Mr Hughson said with a smile that wrinkled up his face. His cheeks were red as if he had spent most of the day outside, and he had ginormous hands.

"Charlie, this is my son, Robert. He's wondering if he can ask you a question about birds. Is that ok? I wouldn't normally ask but he seems rather worried about something or other."

"Of course," said Mr Hughson and he stood up and held out his hand to Robbie.

"Charles Hughson," he stated. "But everyone calls me Charlie."

Robbie shook his hand with a reasonable grip — it was engulfed, but not damaged, by Charlie's enthusiastic greeting.

"Robert — but everyone calls me Robbie."

Charlie released his grip and smiled. "What were you wondering about?"

"Well, the thing is... I found this bird on the beach and it was injured. I didn't know what to do but I ended up bringing it home and putting it in a box. Do you know what I should do now? What will it eat?"

"That would depend on what type of bird it is... can I take a look?" Charlie raised both eyebrows and looked expectantly at Robbie.

"Sure. It's in the porch, just through here."

They both walked in silence back past the herby smells which were escaping from the kitchen. The porch was glass fronted and often warmer than expected on an overcast day. Robbie opened the box and stepped aside to let Charlie peek in. After a couple of seconds, he bent down and gently lifted the bird from its make-shift home. Robbie watched as the older man checked each leg and wing in turn, carefully straightening and folding, stroking and feeling for damaged bones. Every few seconds he would nod to himself. At one point he winced a little and then looked more closely at the bird's plumage.

Robbie waited in silence. He didn't want to frighten the bird or disturb Charlie's concentrated inspection. Besides this, he was not sure what to say anyway. He remained still, hoping for positive news and helpful advice. Charlie eventually sighed, placed the bird carefully back into the box, closed the lid and looked at Robbie.

"This bird is an adult oystercatcher. Its long, straight beak is used to forage for food on the shoreline and in fields – they don't eat oysters though! They are a type of wader so their long legs also help them to paddle in shallow water. Their bold black and white markings are very distinctive, as are their calls which you probably hear regularly – especially if you wander into their territories." Robbie looked down at the box and back to Charlie, hoping for more.

"I'm afraid it appears as though this wee chap has broken a bone in his left wing. This could have been done in a number of ways but it is likely he was hit by a passing car. Apart from this, he is in remarkably good shape. He'll need water and regular feeds; if you are able to give him earthworms, he'd be very grateful as they are one of his favourites. I'm surprised they're not called 'worm catchers' really. Caring for an injured bird is a time commitment and it requires dedication and proper facilities; I have no doubt you can provide the former..." He smiled. "If it's ok with you, I can call my friend and see if he is able to take Mr Oystercatcher in one of his cages. He's a retired vet and very used to this type of request."

Robbie was disappointed at the thought of not being able to nurse the bird back to health himself but it was not a decision about what was best for Robbie.

"Yes, that would be best for him, I would appreciate if you could ask your friend. Is he nearby? Would I be able to visit?" Robbie wondered.

"Well, he's in Shetland but on another island. I will be passing on my way home and will hand the box in to him. I'll leave you his phone number and address, I'm sure you could visit next time you're going to the main town. He always enjoys meeting another animal lover."

"Ok. Good." Robbie smiled. He was an animal lover. But maybe he had only just realised it.

"I'll get a bowl of water and put it in the box Robbie. Could you dig up some worms if I tell you the best way?"

Robbie nodded. He knew it was also time for Charlie's dinner and that he would probably want to eat in peace.

Robbie followed Charlie's instructions exactly. He did not just want a few worms, he wanted loads. He wanted to make sure the oystercatcher was as comfortable and happy as possible while it was in his care.

First, he poured a jug of water on a patch of hidden grass behind the back of the shed. He watched as it soaked down between the blades and darkened the soil. With his wellies back on, he began to jump up and down, stamping and hopping on the wet earth; spade in hand. After a couple of minutes of this strange rain dance, he began to dig. Charlie had explained that this combination of water and tremors would bring the worms to the surface in greater numbers. They liked rain and they would believe by journeying upward they were escaping a burrowing predator which was causing the earth to shake. With old rubber gloves on and a plastic tub at the ready, Robbie was quick to spot his first victims. He would never normally wish to harm any living thing but this was nature at work; the food chain was part of life. Robbie imagined these were the worms the oystercatcher would have eaten if it had not broken its wing.

The grey-pink bodies of the worms twitched and wriggled through the soil and amongst the exposed grass roots, glistening with the damp mud created by Robbie's recent watering. Some were long and thin, others thick and stumpy. He could not even tell which end was the head and which the tail. Do worms have tails? Do they have bones? He did not know.

Robbie could not feel anything through the gloves. After a few seconds of thought, he decided to take them off. He was a little apprehensive; not fearing for his safety, but in recognition of the fact he was not a very tactile person

– there were some textures he did not like. Sometimes Robbie could 'feel' things long after they were gone, he might even dream about them. He was not the type of child who had spent all his nursery sessions in the sand tray or playing with his food.

The worms did not feel as slimy as Robbie had imagined. They moved through the soil with surprising speed – how? He caught the end of one and pulled, gently at first. It had some stretch in it. Its reluctance was obvious but Robbie was resolute and used his free hand to dig around and release the worm from its tunnel. He tightened his grip as the worm made a determined effort to find darkness and safety; it was clearly boneless, an invertebrate. Robbie dropped the worm into his container and quickly began grabbing and digging before the other worms had a chance to disappear. He had no idea how many worms the oystercatcher needed but it was up to Robbie to ensure it had enough strength to repair its wing and make a full recovery.

Twenty minutes (and two damp, dug-up patches of ground) later, Robbie had half-filled his tub and completely eradicated his worm-touch trepidation. The next question was how to feed his patient – should he give all the worms at once, feed them one at a time into the bird's beak or mix them with earth and scatter them in the bottom of the bird's new home? Logic dictated that, in nature, the oystercatcher would find and gobble one worm every few minutes. Robbie did not want to emulate this process exactly, having done the digging to save the bird from having to use precious energy or injure itself further. Instead he decided to drop a few worms into the bird's box at regular intervals until they were finished. He was fully prepared to dig for more then or even try looking under rocks for other insects to see if the oystercatcher liked them. Maybe it did not like to eat bones or legs, as neither oysters nor worms had these. On this basis, slugs might make a substitute snack, Robbie deduced.

Despite enjoying a delicious meal, fit for humans, Charlie had found time to put a bowl of water in the oystercatcher's box. Robbie dropped in five live, wriggling worms. The bird poked at them with its beak and, within seconds, they were gone.

For the rest of the evening Robbie stayed close to the bird box, regularly feeding the casualty, researching information online and looking at bird books with Charlie. Robbie found it all fascinating and could relate a lot of what he was reading with the habitat and species he had seen on his walks – it was becoming real. Charlie answered most of Robbie's questions with ease but Robbie preferred to try to find the answers for himself, and so much of the time they spent together was quiet though not awkward. This was a new experience for Robbie; it was nice to spend time with someone he admired. He was surprised how interesting it was to study and learn, and it was reassuring to enjoy a comfortable silence.

CHAPTER FIVE

At the Bed and Breakfast the washing machine always seemed to be mid-cycle. Sheets and towels were always billowing on the clothes line and delicious smells always seemed to emanate from the kitchen.

Morning was an especially busy time. Robbie was tired; he had woken in the middle of the night and come to check on the oystercatcher. After that he had difficulty getting back to sleep again. Towards summer, the nights in Shetland were famously light. This far north the sun only dipped below the horizon for a matter of hours and the problem would only get worse until after the summer solstice in June. Ruth was going to make blackout curtains to help combat the incoming brightness but, for the time being, she was too busy to attend to them. She had a long and extending list of jobs both in and outside the Bed and Breakfast – jobs her husband would have been more than happy to help with. It also didn't help that in the night, Robbie's thoughts always became darker; even if his room did not.

When the fantasy of being able to eat bacon, eggs and sausage every morning actually became a reality, Robbie found he just did not have the appetite for it day after day. Cereal had a new appeal to him, as long as he ate it before it became too soggy. As usual he read the box that sat in front of him and wondered what all the ingredients were. He looked at the bright colours and cartoon characters. His mother was right; it was a wasted opportunity – if the packaging had been printed with times tables and passages from classic literature, he would have read them. There was something about cereal boxes on kitchen tables in early mornings that resulted in a captivated audience, an audience usually eating and reading brightly coloured, cheap junk.

Robbie did not usually get up quite this early as he hadn't started back at school yet, but Charlie had mentioned he was intending on making the most of his last day on Unst, and Robbie did not want to miss his departure. Ruth was busy serving and chatting in the dining room. On the radio, the news headlines and weather bulletins were repeated at regular intervals, although the traffic updates were no longer relevant Robbie thought.

As he finished his cereal and rinsed his dish, Robbie moved towards the sparsely filled fruit bowl. Fresh fruit was not always available on Unst, and Ruth had started to use the bowl as a dumping ground for all the little bits of shrapnel associated with moving house and having a growing son. The usual coins, Allen keys and microwave instructions were hidden under a pile of objects that Ruth had removed from Robbie's muddy trouser pockets. She knew not to throw away even the scrunched-up tissues – having learned the hard way that they may contain some fragile 'treasure' picked up on one of Robbie's nature walks.

Today the collection included a few shells, some nuggets of sea-worn glass, a bit of dried seaweed and two crab claws. Robbie's attention moved to the stones he had gathered the day before. A couple of them looked less impressive than he remembered, having now dried and dimmed. He picked up his new favourite, drained the bottom of the orange juice carton and went to find Charlie.

"Ah, here's the wee David Attenborough now." Charlie turned to greet Robbie. "How are you this morning?"

"I am ok. How do you think the bird is?" Robbie wondered aloud, anxiously.

"He looks stronger to me. I will be taking him today – I'm sure he'll make a good recovery. What are your plans?"

"I'm not sure," said Robbie. "I might have to help mum, but I have three questions before you go, if you have time..."

"You've been mulling over what we were reading about yesterday, perhaps? Ask! Ask! I have eaten my breakfast far too quickly, as usual, so I have time, of course I have time." With a flourish Charlie settled again in a leather chair and folded his arms over his satisfied belly.

"I was wondering what a 'raptor' is."

"You're very observant," noted Charlie. His Fife Raptor Group hat was now sitting on the front seat of his hire car. "A raptor is a bird of prey. Many birds eat prey, as you know, but this really refers to the king hunters – eagles, falcons and hawks – that type of thing. They are the killing machines, adapted to precision hunt, to dive like a speeding bullet, to tear and grab prey almost hidden in the undergrowth. Watching them at work is watching nature at its most effective." Charlie's eyes lit up with passion and excitement when he spoke about raptors. He seemed to love everything about them, from their plumage and feather shape to their acute senses and flying techniques. "Waders and seabirds are interesting too," he conceded, "but raptors are my favourite. I encourage you to learn more about them."

"There are so many more birds to learn about than I expected. In Harrow I wasn't that interested because I really only saw pigeons and starlings. There were some brighter ones at the park sometimes but I didn't pay much attention back then and I haven't seen them in Shetland, I don't think. What about the trees? There are hardly any here."

"There are a combination of factors which account for the lack of trees in Shetland. These include the salty air, the wind – record speeds have been recorded up here in winter time – and the lack of suitable soil depth. There are also grazing animals which often damage the saplings people plant. Shetland plants are usually hardy and low lying. The only trees you will find here are in sheltered areas, possibly in a gully, and often within a walled garden. The Shetland people are not used to trees so they don't really miss them. They enjoy seeing to the far horizon without trees blocking their view to the sea. You can see the sea from almost everywhere in Shetland, and there are some beautiful and unusual flowers here if you are interested in plants."

"Lastly, I was wondering if you knew what this is?" Robbie held out his hand and passed Mr Hughson his favourite pebble from yesterday's beachcomb.

"Hmmmm. Now this is where my limited expertise will get the better of me. Geology is not my strong point, Robbie. But I know just the man for the job and I'm heading that way, if you care to join me."

"Is it far?" asked Robbie. "I'll have to check with mum..." Ruth would never have allowed Robbie to go anywhere with a stranger in London, but Charlie had relations on Unst, he could only leave the island by ferry, and Ruth had all his details on her booking form.

Ruth spoke to Charlie about the plans as Robbie waited in the hall, watching through the glass door panels. Ruth's head nodded and she pointed and gesticulated with her hands but Robbie could not tell what she was saying as her back was turned. Charlie's face looked smiley and free of tension. Out of Robbie's earshot, he was telling Ruth about a kind, old man who used to be the school's caretaker. Ruth turned and signalled for Robbie to come back in.

"Right, Charlie's going to take you down the road to see a man about your stone but he'll have to leave you there to visit his family before catching the ferry. You can walk home, but I'll come and get you if it starts raining. Charlie will take the bird with him now too. Is that all ok?"

Robbie nodded. He wondered where they were going.

A few minutes later Robbie and Charlie pulled up to a large, flat building opposite the local church. Most buildings were flat in Shetland, Robbie could not remember seeing one over three storeys. The building seemed reasonably new, it was made of modern materials and was in excellent condition with no sign of weather damage. The window frames were red and the landscaped gardens around the car park were starting to flower.

"This is Nordagarth, the local care centre," Charlie clarified. "My uncle stayed here for a long time and so I know the staff. I like to visit them when I'm on Unst and they have introduced me to some of the residents. One of them, Jack, will be able to help you with your stone. Let's meet him."

Robbie looked around. He wasn't sure what he'd expected, but it wasn't this. It seemed to be some kind of old folks' home. He was sure it would smell.

"Hey Charlie, you're up again. Good to see you. Who is your friend?" called a man as they walked in.

Charlie caught-up with staff and told them of the mission. Robbie took in his surroundings. The main foyer was bright and airy, full of glass and plants but no bad smells. The main hall led to a communal sitting area and, when the doors swung open, Robbie could see lots of framed artwork and a large television.

"Come through," said Charlie. "Jack's playing cards by the sounds of it."

At a table near the windows sat an elderly man with a tartan blanket over his lap. His wispy, white hair was rather windswept and gave him the appearance of a mad professor. His hands shook as he turned over large playing cards and placed them on to piles with some strategy in mind.

"Jack! How good to see you. You're looking well. Still playing patience I see..."

The two men chatted and Robbie was introduced. He stood quietly and listened. Jack's face was full of wrinkles and experiences. His skin was marked and veiny in places and his eyes were slightly milky but they shone as he laughed with Charlie and spoke about times gone by.

After a few minutes Charlie had to leave. He promised Robbie he would deliver the bird safely to its new home and would keep in touch. Charlie seemed to know a lot of people around here – he had a friend for every occasion.

The oldest person Robbie could remember speaking with was his granddad, his father's father. All his other grandparents had died while Robbie was a small child. His granddad had been quite ill at the time and had died shortly afterwards. Robbie could not remember what they had said but Ruth had done most of the talking.

Robbie was now alone with Jack. A man who looked about a hundred. A man who knew about stones.

CHAPTER SIX

"When I was your age I didn't drink tea," Jack admitted, "I grew to love it though, it was my petrol. I'm not allowed too much these days. Would you like to have some with me?"

Robbie felt it would be rude to say no, despite Jack's kind attempt not to pressure him.

"I'll try some, if that's ok."

Jack spoke to a lady in a navy-blue tabard and she shortly appeared with tea, milk and sugar.

"Charlie's a very nice man. I have known him probably longer than you've been alive." Jack stirred his sugary tea and tapped the spoon on the edge of his own special cup. "I hope I can help you with your stone, son. Can I see it?"

Robbie took the stone out of his pocket, passed it to Jack and sat on a neighbouring high-backed armchair. The old man rubbed and turned the stone in his bony fingers and tried to scratch it with the edge of his teaspoon. It was not as silvery or layered as some of the other stones Robbie had found but he had been attracted by its smooth green colour.

"This is serpentine," Jack told him. "It's a beautiful piece Robbie, well done for finding it. I used to polish stones – this one would look lovely after a few days of tumbling." He passed it to Robbie and sat back with his strangely small teacup in one hand, slurping periodically. The tea was still far too hot for Robbie's novice lips. He had added milk but could still see coils of steam spiralling off its surface.

"I don't get as many visitors as I'd like. It's nice for me to see young people for a change. You still have more ahead of you than behind you." He smiled and looked out the window towards the bay.

"This village used to be a bustling herring port, you know?" he said. "There used to be so many boats they almost filled the distance from the shore to that smaller island." Jack indicated with his finger where the fishing boats would have moored. "This village nearly became the capital town of Shetland. It would have been very different if that had happened."

"My dad liked to go fishing, if he had time. He used a rod though," Robbie found himself saying.

"He'll like it here then, there are lots of places to fish in the lochs or in the sea. He could join the Angling Club."

"He's not here. It's just me and my mum." There was a pause. Jack looked at Robbie. He knew not to ask any more about it. Time and experience had taught him that people tell their stories only when they are ready.

"Does your mother like flowers?" Jack asked, brightly.

Robbie nodded.

"Over on that hill – behind the road to the garage – there is a unique habitat. The soil is poor and covered with little stones; it almost looks like a lunar landscape. Later in the year a small, white flower appears there; a kind of chickweed. A special kind; it grows there and nowhere else. Nowhere else in the whole world. It's protected but you can go and look at it."

Robbie felt the hairs on his neck stand up. He imagined taking his mum to see such rare flowers. It was an unusual opportunity; a chance to make her smile. She deserved it.

Jack spoke to Robbie for a long time. They discussed history and the community, and change. When Jack was Robbie's age he was already working; doing the first of his many jobs. He had witnessed things Robbie's generation could never understand, and had grown up in a time when the technological advances that Robbie took for granted were not even in their infancy. How could a man adjust to such changes in just a few decades?

"In my day," he reminisced, "I think life was simpler than you have it today. We may not have had all the gadgets you have, but the world felt like a smaller place. I always enjoyed being outdoors, working with my hands and making things. We wouldn't have had time to sit on phones or computers all day, even if they'd been invented. Today, there's just too much going on for my liking. People never seem satisfied with what they have now."

"You're a young man Robbie. It's different when you're young," said Jack. "I used to drive fast cars to feel alive, now I can feel just as excited playing 'snap'."

A shaft of unexpected sunlight settled on Robbie's face. The room fell silent, and the two new friends watched as silver-edged clouds were blown swiftly over the brightening sun. Flickering sunbeams shimmered as they danced towards the fields and fences. On the horizon, full, grey clouds threatened rain behind glistening rays which lit random waves breaking under their natural spotlight. Brightness streamed cheerfully into the recreation room, creating moving patterns on the carpet. Jack's watch face sent a glowing reflection onto the nearby wallpaper where it sparkled like a fire fly. A minute later the area dimmed and, although the moment was over, it held the room mesmerised for a further few seconds of awe.

Spending time with a much older person was a new experience for Robbie. Jack had done so much but felt no need to boast about it. He seemed content. He was not nosey, but somehow got Robbie to speak.

"When you're young, you feel invincible. You young people don't think about mortality much," said Jack.

"I do," admitted Robbie. He looked down at his cold tea. "How can you enjoy life if you are worried about dying? How can you care about people when something might happen to them?"

"Robbie," Jack waited until he had the boy's gaze again, "when I lost my wife, I was devastated and felt lost but that's not what she would have wanted. We don't live forever, that's what makes life so precious and special. In some ways, I feel luckier as I get older. Each sunset seems more beautiful because I pay more attention, in case I don't get the chance again."

Robbie was able to understand a little of what Jack meant. He had seen birds and plants before but never really looked. Or heard. Or smelled. Or touched. Life in Harrow had been rushed. He had been focussed on impressing his friends. He had thought he knew it all.

"People can't know it all," Jack laughed when they discussed it. "Start by trying to know yourself. What makes you 'you' Robbie?"

Robbie knew he was not as happy as he ought to be. He knew his mother was worried about him and he knew that sometimes life seemed overwhelming. But Unst was turning out to be a place of simplicity and companionship. He could see possibilities – the possibility of feeling more peaceful, the possibility of making new friends.

The old man was getting tired. He could barely remember the last time he had spoken at such length.

"Jack, I have liked talking with you today. Would it be ok to visit again?" Robbie asked.

"I have a better idea," Jack said with a glint in his eye. "The church has a sale and auction in the village hall tomorrow night and I would like to go but I would need a bit of help. I can ask the staff about it. They will take me there and bring me back if you want to come along."

"What time?"

"Could you be here at 1830 hours?"

"Six-thirty?" Robbie smiled. "Yes, I will be here. And one day you'll have to teach me how to play cards too!"

Robbie picked his serpentine off the table and gave the lady the cups and plates.

"I'll see you tomorrow Jack – 1830 hours. Thank you for today."

Robbie slept well that night. He felt calmer, appreciated and listened to. Ruth had enjoyed hearing about her son's afternoon – she believed it was important that Robbie had male role-models in his life and that he met people of different ages, with different life experiences to share.

The following evening Robbie and Ruth went to the care centre to accompany Jack to the sale and auction. All the money raised was going towards a new church roof and most of the community was expected to be there. Ruth felt it was an opportunity to meet new people on the island and help Robbie integrate better. Robbie introduced her to Jack. The old man had combed his hair and put on a bright, knitted sweater for his evening out. It looked a bit like the one Charlie had worn.

"It's lovely to meet you Jack. Robbie told me you boys had some very interesting discussions yesterday. Thank you for taking time to answer his questions. We're both very happy to have your expert help at the auction this evening; neither of us have been to one before."

"My dear Ruth, the pleasure is mine. I could not manage on my own these days."

At the village hall, Ruth and Robbie helped Jack out of the care home minibus. Ruth held his arm as Robbie opened the doors. There were already a lot of people in the hall and the car park was almost full. After paying a small donation at the door and buying some raffle tickets, Ruth sat on a bench with Jack while Robbie walked around the trestle tables which were laden with items, old and new. Small children ran around and adults talked. At 7pm the Laird's wife welcomed everyone, and declared the sale open as the crowd clapped. Jack began speaking to two men so Ruth and Robbie had a look at the book stall. Robbie bought a nature book which had sections about birds, plants, animals and insects. He walked around with Ruth as she introduced herself to people and bought some soap and a mug holder. Robbie had a look at the items on the stage which were going to be sold to the highest bidder in the auction. He knew what he wanted.

Jack sat on the bench and spoke with various locals. Robbie sat next to him and looked at his new book, trying to learn the names of some waders. Just before the auction, the stall tables were cleared away by ladies from the SWRI (Robbie was not sure what that was) and other people filled the hall with additional rows of benches. Once everyone was seated, the SWRI ladies brought in tea, coffee and trays of sandwiches and cakes. Robbie helped Jack with his half-filled teacup and his plate, and took some orange squash for himself. Ruth brought her purchases and sat down beside them. Before long a man walked on to the stage, another held up the first item and the auction began.

CHAPTER SEVEN

The first item to be auctioned was a hand crocheted blanket which got the bidding going at a rapid pace. "10, 12, 15, 18, 20, 22... any more bids? Come on, a lovely warm thing, it's taken a lot of time and skill to make, let's see some generosity... £22 any advance on £22?"

After some laughter and encouragement the blanket sold for £35. It was followed by a box of seed potatoes, an old doll's house then an Eastern style candle holder.

Jack tried for a painting for his room but he was outbid by some holiday-makers. Ruth bought a chip and vegetable chopping set, which Robbie was under strict instructions never to touch.

Next came a potted geranium in flower. It caught Jack's eye.

"Robbie, will you bid for me?" Jack asked.

"How much is your maximum?" Robbie needed to know.

"I haven't decided yet, let's see what happens," said Jack.

The auctioneer started items at a price he thought was fair. Robbie looked to Jack for guidance.

"A lovely red geranium, a good few weeks of flowering on her yet. Nice smell from the leaves, healthy. Comes in the blue, ceramic pot... who'll give me £5 for it?"

Jack gave a slight shake of his head; this meant 'hold on, he'll drop the starting price'.

"£2 – you couldn't even buy the pot for that in the shops."

Jack looked at Robbie and dipped his chin. Robbie's hand shot straight up.

"£2 I'm bid. From the young gardener near the back. Good man. Who'll give me 3?"

The bidding continued one pound at a time. Jack would nod or nudge Robbie's elbow if he wanted the boy to bid. It was quite exciting. After a few minutes Jack won the plant for £11 and a man brought it to him and collected his money.

It was a lot for a plant, but Jack told Robbie it was really a contribution to the church roof.

"I don't want it leaking during my funeral," he joked. Robbie had not known how to respond to that, he did not want to think about it.

After about forty minutes more sandwiches, biscuits and cakes were brought around and the auctioneer announced that the raffle would be drawn. Ruth removed the yellow tickets from her pocket and handed them to Robbie. He looked at them. Numbers 120–124. Jack had blue tickets 35–39. Jack said he had his eye on the bottles of alcohol, although he wasn't allowed to drink them. Robbie was more hopeful for the large tin of chocolates, and Ruth would have liked the lavender powder, soap and body lotion set.

"Pink number 128... Blue number 3... Blue again, number 97..."

On this occasion luck was not on their side. Robbie had enjoyed the anticipation nevertheless and clapped with Jack when a lady who worked at the care home won the chocolates. He also recognised a man he had seen working in the bakery and the doctor (who seemed pleased to win a bottle of red wine).

The auction resumed and it was not long before the item Robbie had been waiting for was held up.

"We have here – how shall we describe these? Vintage? Retro? ... Old?" The audience laughed. "We have here an old pair of binoculars in their original leather case. I can assure you that, despite their rather battered appearance, I have checked them and they are in perfect working order. They have a manual focus and 10 x magnification, and are made by a reputable manufacturer... binoculars. Good things.

Useful for looking at the birds or spying on the neighbours... who'll start me at £5?" The laughter died down. Everyone knew what would happen, so they waited.

"£3 then, I'm not starting lower... £3 I'm bid, £4, £5..."

Robbie was disappointed. The price had gone up quickly and he only had £8 left. He looked anxious. Suddenly Jack held his wrist and raised both their arms together.

"£6... £7... £8..."

Robbie bid one more time, he was at his maximum now.

"£9... Any advance on £9?"

Jack looked at Ruth. She smiled.

"£10... £11..."

Robbie sighed. Someone else had a bigger budget and he couldn't match it. It was easy to get carried away but Robbie had counted his coins umpteen times and his total never increased. He turned to his mother with a look of disappointment.

"£11, going once, going twice... £12! New bidder..."

Robbie had stopped paying attention. He looked at the cover of his book and decided he wanted to go home.

"£12... I'm selling at twelve... fair warning... sold! Sold to Jack Spence... Jack – are these for bird watching or neighbour watching?"

"They are for my new friend, the young David Attenborough here. Robbie is a keen ornithologist." There was a small ripple of applause and Jack was brought the binoculars as he handed over his money. Robbie did not know what to say.

"Jack, that's too generous. Thank you so much!" Ruth said. Robbie nodded, shyly.

"It's alright, son. I can't take this money with me, after all. You can come and tell what you see with them. I'd enjoy that." He handed Robbie the binoculars.

"That really is very kind Jack. You didn't need to do that," added Ruth.

The old man smiled a contented smile.

"I'm ready to go when you are," he said.

The notice in the shop thanked the local community for being so supportive of the sale and auction event. It announced that £1814 had been raised for the church roof. It thanked the Scottish Women's Rural Institute for the tea and cakes; Robbie knew who they were now. Jack was very pleased when he heard the news – it was a lot of money for a small community to raise. Robbie was happy he had played his part too. People recognised him now and said hello when they saw him out walking – always with his binoculars around his neck.

Robbie tried to make the most of the next few days. He explored the old ruined building near his home, observed the pond life that inhabited the pool in the nearby field and set up a nature table in his room, complete with drawing area, magnifying glass, new book and empty tubs for collecting specimens. He had a box filled with seeds, feathers, shells and dead insects – most of which came from inside the shed or on window ledges. If he had successfully identified a sample by looking in his new book or online, he stuck it on a piece of cardboard and labelled it.

All too soon the holidays were over and Robbie had to start going to the local Junior High School. He had been told that the school system was different. There was not a huge number of children his age on the island and he knew it would be a change from his class of 30 in Harrow.

Ruth brought Robbie to school in the car today but, until autumn, he would walk or cycle as mornings would be busy at the Bed and Breakfast. The school door had a huge mosaic next to it, showing important places and objects from the local area. Different industries, wildlife and locations were represented. The door led to a large glass porch filled with seats and lockers. Music was playing. The area seemed to have been hijacked by the oldest children and was used as a type of common room. Various bags and coats had been left haphazardly on the floor – items that would have been stolen if this had been Harrow. It seemed very relaxed but you could tell it was safe and clean.

Inside another door Ruth found the reception on the right. She spoke to the school administrator and filled in paperwork. The phone rang, the photocopier churned out maps and question sheets, and another lady sat counting money as she waited for a laminator machine to heat up.

Robbie looked into the centre of the school where a large multi-purpose hall was being filled with tables and chairs in preparation for lunch. Something smelled scrumptious. Robbie thought it might be roast chicken. On every available wall, notice boards were filled with mounted art work and photographs. This was the secondary department; rooms coming off the main corridor were signed 'Physics', 'French' and 'English'. Around the hall was the art department, technical workshop, staff room, kitchens and the head teacher's office.

A few children walked around. They didn't wear a uniform. It seemed they could wear whatever they wanted – any style and colour. This was something entirely new to Robbie. Ruth had already bought him some black school trousers and various sweatshirts as she told him she did not want him coming to school in jeans or taking half an hour deciding what to wear in the mornings.

The receptionist came out of her office and began to show Ruth and Robbie around before Robbie joined his class.

"It's nice to meet you Robbie, I'm Miss McIntosh. We'll start in the primary department because a couple of rooms there are used by the secondary department; social subjects have been relocated and there is access to the school green houses, vegetable gardens and pond. The home economics, health and PHSE lessons take place upstairs, along with maths and science, in the lab. The booklet I have given you will tell you about times, rules and routines. If you have any questions, please ask."

Miss McIntosh had obviously given this tour many times before. Although it was a small school it was still confusing to a newcomer and Robbie felt a little overwhelmed. Ruth was impressed with the resources – there were large fields for outdoor play, a separate nursery and music block and a well-equipped computer suite. The primary department was made up of composite classes, and secondary year groups were small but individual. Some exam level classes only contained two or three children which meant there was a lot of teacher attention and the curriculum was covered quickly and in depth. Most children, according to Miss McIntosh, behaved well, worked hard and enjoyed extra-curricular activities such as sports, music and youth clubs.

Robbie's class stayed together, followed a timetable and had not yet started focussing on exam work. There were eight periods in the day with a morning and lunch break. He was given a list of his teacher's names and a timetable.

"Time to meet your class," Miss McIntosh informed them. "Can you tell me where they ought to be at the moment, Robbie?"

Robbie looked at his watch and the timetable.

"They are in the middle of double maths, upstairs in the lab," he said.

The maths room had a wall of south facing windows which made it quite warm. Seven children sat at long tables facing an interactive white board. There were three girls and four boys. They turned to face the door when the trio arrived.

"Sorry to interrupt, Mr Taylor. This is Robbie, he'll be joining this class. His file is in the office should you wish to see it. Can we leave him in your capable hands?"

"Of course, thank you. Welcome Robbie, take a seat. Mel, can you get Robbie the workbook and textbooks he'll need please?"

"Enjoy your day, see you later," said Ruth, carefully trying not to embarrass her son. She left with Miss McIntosh.

Robbie sat at a desk between the door and another boy and the lesson began again as if he had always been there.

CHAPTER EIGHT

As Robbie settled into the school term, his initial visit to Jack became the first of many. Robbie had to interview a local person for a class project and Jack had agreed to help. It was not all work though, Robbie also learned how to play cards and dominoes.

One Thursday Robbie decided that, straight after his next appointment with Dr Hawkins, he would go to visit Jack. Robbie brought his nature book. He wanted to show Jack which species he had spotted around the island.

"I am impressed with this book," concluded Jack. "It has most of the information you need to start your nature studies."

"I have seen curlew and snipe this week. They are making lots of noise up on the hills." Robbie gave his updates.

"Yes, they will be displaying at this time. How's school going?"

"It's ok, I suppose. Sometimes it's a bit boring. Most of the time we are not studying things that I'm very interested in. I don't know why we need to learn about stuff that's of no real use."

"You're learning how to learn, that's the main thing. It's hard to know what might be useful in the future at your age." Jack told him.

"What do you mean?"

"Well, you're learning skills like not giving up, and making yourself do things, even if you can't be bothered. Working at a job is sometimes boring, but you just have to get on with it, or else... School is meant to get you ready for the real world. I guess at school your teacher is like your boss."

"Hmmmm," said Robbie. He'd need more convincing.

"You'll get to do more of the things you like if you work hard and show you're reliable when you're first getting started. First impressions, and all that. You don't want your boss to think you're lazy and just want to do the fun stuff."

'But I am quite lazy and I do just want to do the fun stuff...' thought Robbie. 'Work plus paying bills and taxes; being a grown up sounded a bit rubbish.' Although he pretended he wanted to get on with being a man, inside he kind of wished he could just stay a kid forever and have no responsibilities. He wondered if grown men were allowed to still live with their mums and get all their cooking and washing done for them. He knew Jack would really disapprove of this kind of thinking.

"Make sure you get your life skills too, Robbie. Like accepting that sometimes people will have different ideas from yours. And, for goodness sake, make sure you've got a good handshake; no-one likes a wet fish... Always make eye contact. Smile. Unless you're at a funeral." Jack laughed.

Robbie was not sure what he was laughing at, but it seemed to be a memory.

"If you learn how to learn," Jack continued, "you can then use the same techniques at home to study whatever you are interested in." He sat back, closed his eyes and let out a sigh. Robbie could only presuppose that Jack had had some very good and some very poor teachers during his short time in formal education. He had already told Robbie about numerous times when he had been given the cane, or the belt, at school.

"You learned a lot about this even though you left school very young," Robbie observed.

"I'm afraid I did not learn these lessons until much later in life, when I found teachers in the army, in the community, in my work. There are teachers everywhere. I did not make the most of my schooling opportunities and that is why I spent a lot of time in trouble." He paused. "Now, tell me about that classmate you don't like…"

"Sarah?"

"Sarah. Tell me about her… What's she done now?" Jack smiled. For all his guru-tendencies, he still liked a regular chinwag now and again. Robbie was thankful; there were moments in his conversations with Jack where he felt overloaded. He did not have enough time to process all that Jack said. If anyone else had said it, Robbie would not have even been interested enough to listen, but Jack had lived a life, learned things the hard way and he had earned Robbie's respect.

Robbie had, slowly, begun to almost like very weak tea. As they chatted about school, Robbie enjoyed a second cup – predominantly as an excuse to eat another biscuit and put off doing his homework for a little longer.

"Why do you drink tea from such a teenie cup?" he asked Jack.

"Well, I have kidney failure," said his elder friend, very casually. Robbie looked surprised and wanted to know more. Jack explained that, normally, kidneys cleaned out extra chemicals from the body but that his waterworks were more like water-not-works. Because of this, he could only drink a very limited amount of fluid.

He told Robbie that he had to go to hospital three times each week for dialysis. During dialysis Jack was attached to a machine which took the extra toxins out of his blood – to do the job his kidneys couldn't. He also said he could not eat certain foods if they contained lots of the 'bad guys'.

"So, that's why I have the peerie cups," he concluded. It all sounded pretty bionic to Robbie and he didn't know what 'peerie' meant, but he was too scared to ask, in case it was something to do with 'waterworks'… Eugh.

As Jack had finished his tea first, he absentmindedly flicked through the nature book as they spoke. He stopped, mid-sentence, when the book lay with its cover open.

"Look here," said Jack. He pointed to a name written neatly with the blue ink of a fountain pen. The old fashioned, joined-up handwriting read Beth M. Wishart. This clearly captured Jack's imagination. "I wonder who she was," he pondered. "I wonder what she used this book for."

Robbie ran his finger over the signature. It was a puzzle. A bit of a mystery.

"I think we might be able to find out who she is." Robbie smiled.

"We? How can we do that?"

"Well, we could maybe just ask Charlie – he probably knows her...!" The two laughed. "No," said Robbie, "really, I think we could try to look her up on the Internet. Remember I told you about that? It's like the biggest library in the world, on the computer. It is an amazing tool if you can use it efficiently. I could show you and we could do it together, if you like?"

"Son, that ship sailed without me, I am afraid. They tried to show us computers in here but I couldn't get the hang of it. I tried to type but I could have written it three times quicker and with fewer mistakes. Those machines seem to be for lazy, younger people that can't write or spell or learn things from books. Most people just seem to play games or look at pictures of places they should go and see in real life." Jack suddenly looked old, judgemental and unimpressed. It was not like him.

"You sound like a quitter to me. What about 'lifelong-learning' and doing things, even if you're not very interested in them?" said Robbie. The old man raised his eyebrows, tilted his head to the side and pursed his lips. He knew he had painted himself into this corner.

"You do it. I'll watch," Jack compromised.

The following Saturday Robbie returned to the care home. He had brought his laptop and set it up in the sitting area after checking with staff how to access the Wi-Fi system. He gave Jack the nature book. The computer was online.

"The first thing to do is to get to a page where you can type in what you want to find out about. This type of page is called a 'Search Engine' – it is a bit like the index of a book but you have to be more specific." Robbie typed 'How to wash a dog' into Google. A list of pages appeared.

"If I'd just typed 'dog', we would have spent ages trying to find out how to wash one. But here, you can see lots of instructions. Although you have to be aware that some are from people at home writing whatever they want – they could lie or give you information that is not recommended. The best sites to look at are more official. See this one?" Robbie pointed at the screen. "This is the British Dog Association website. That's where I would go to if I wanted to wash a dog correctly."

"Well, I don't have a dog. So, what about Beth? Can we just type in her name? Won't lots of people with the same name show on the screen?" It was a good question.

Robbie felt the tables were turned – he was teaching Jack, for a change, and it was interesting to see the older man in the role of student.

"Yes, we need to find out something else, if we can. If she got the book when it was new, we can find out when it was printed and that would give us a date. We can also guess how old she might have been when she got the book and that will give us her approximate year of birth. You are happier with books – look through and see if you can find any clues," Robbie instructed.

Jack looked through the front of the book to find the printer and publisher information. This was the third edition of the book, printed in 1974. As he flicked through the pages, something fluttered out onto the table.

"What's this?" Jack asked, picking up the piece of paper. It was a newspaper page about a rare bird sighting. At the top of the page was printed Aberdeen Gazette, 14 May 1974. Jack read the article.

"... Eighteen-year-old student Elizabeth Wishart first spotted the rare warbler while out walking with her father, an amateur ornithologist..."

"We got lucky finding that!" said Robbie. He opened the computer's calculator and tried to work out a birthdate. "This means our Beth Wishart was born between May 1955 and May 1956. If she was 18, she was probably studying somewhere in Aberdeen. Let's try that."

Robbie typed his key words in to the Google search – Elizabeth M. Wishart, Aberdeen University, 1974. Within a few seconds a list of possible sites appeared. Robbie clicked on the first one as Jack looked on, amazed.

"This one lists enrolments and exams sat at Aberdeen University. In the class of 1974 there was an Elizabeth Mary Wishart studying zoology. I think that is her. The second entry is another article about the bird she found and this third one... I don't think it's relevant; it is an article about Elizabeth LaRocca and Bryan Wishart from Aberdeen, Texas."

Robbie typed in 'Elizabeth Wishart, Aberdeen, 1956'.

"There was an Elizabeth Mary Wishart born in Aberdeen hospital in January 1956 to William and Theresa Wishart. I wonder if that's her?"

"I think it is!" said Jack, excitedly. "It said in the newspaper that her dad was called Bill, which is short for William."

Robbie was pleased. He felt he had persuaded Jack of the values of the Internet. He picked up his nature book and looked at the signature again.

"This book," he said, in summary, "belonged to Elizabeth Mary Wishart. She was known as 'Beth'. We know where and when she was born and the name of her parents. We know she used this book to help her get her zoology qualification at Aberdeen University in 1974, when she was 18. If I had more time, we could probably find out more and try to link her to Shetland, to see why the book is here now."

"I enjoyed that and I can see some of the advantages of the modern technology," Jack conceded. "I wonder if there's anything about me on the Internet?"

And with that, Robbie knew Jack had been converted.

CHAPTER NINE

At the north end of the island was a large nature reserve leading to cliffs and a lighthouse, these were at the very top of the British Isles. According to Jack the lighthouse, Muckle Flugga, had been designed and built by Robert Louis Stevenson's father and uncle. The author had spent time on Unst during this period and it was here he had, allegedly, first conjured up his famous tale, Treasure Island. On hearing that the map in the famous book bore some resemblance to that of Unst, Ruth had bought Robbie a copy and he was reading it frantically.

The nature reserve of Hermaness was home to thousands upon thousands of seabirds. The colonies formed a significant percentage of the world's population of gannets, guillemots and puffins. Jack described the sounds and smells in great detail but this fell short of seeing it for himself and Ruth had promised Robbie she would take him. The cliffs were unforgiving and she knew, while Robbie watched the birds, she would have to watch the excitable Robbie. It was something to look forward to in the summer months – a picnic, maybe a wander along one of the sandy beaches. He would take photos on his phone camera.

Robbie tried to learn some information about the seabirds before his visit. He wanted to know what typical behaviours to observe, what nesting sites to look for and what plumage. On the Internet he could watch video clips and hear calls, but nothing could possibly compare to the real thing. The warden might even give a guided walk and answer some of Robbie's many questions. He might lead them past the infamous attacking great skuas as they tried to protect their nest sites.

To compensate for his Hermaness wait, Ruth agreed to let Robbie visit another northern area; Lambaness. She attached Robbie's bike to her car's roof rack and dropped him off with a bag of sandwiches, crisps, juice and chocolate. The cycle home would be mostly downhill, Ruth had saved him the hard work.

"Now, you're sure you're allowed to be here?" she had asked.

"Jack says all the local kids come here now and then," Robbie had reassured her.

And here he was, at the end of the long, bumpy, single-track road. He cycled for about a third of a mile. The road went down at a steep angle and then rose again at the end, like a ski-jump. His bike accelerated to a rapid pace but Robbie controlled it with the brakes – this was not a social hot-spot, even a cyclist with a protective mother could be left lying injured for hours. He left his bike at the side of the track on some heather.

Lambaness was owned by the Ministry of Defence, or MOD. It was a mysterious part of the RAF base, which Robbie's Uncle Chris had mentioned to Robbie on the phone.

There was a chance that Robbie was not really meant to be wandering around Lambaness but the structures he could see had been left to ruin and the area was unmanned. There was only one fenced off area and he had no intention of exploring that. There had been no gate across the road. There were just a couple of visible buildings and some strange shapes protruding from the grass and heather. As he walked closer he could see dark concrete entrances leading underground. What a strange place.

During the Cold War, Lambaness had been an observation post. A place where camouflaged radar and hidden primitive computer systems would have gathered data and been on the lookout for enemies. Jack had told Robbie to find a large, circular pool which, he insisted, had been formed in the crater of a dropped bomb. It was not immediately obvious. Robbie had decided to explore the furthest end first and work his way back to his bike, ready to journey home. He had brought his torch and his penknife, just in case, a bag for any nature collecting and his phone. He walked past the buildings, and numerous confused sheep, and made his way to a circular wall, about shoulder height, at the far end of the complex.

The concrete wall created an almost unbroken circle about three metres in diameter. Robbie entered it through the one gap in the circumference. This had once been the location of a mounted anti-aircraft gun. It was easy to see why; from this position, allies would have had an uninterrupted view of the seas and skies for hundreds of miles to the east. Early warning could be given for any incoming attack. Robbie could see only sea and horizon for over 180 degrees; so vast was the expanse of water, he could actually detect the curvature of the Earth itself. The horizon was no longer completely straight but bent around until it touched, at either end, more cliffs and treeless islands forming the rugged Shetland coast. Robbie stood and imagined seeing enemy aircraft approaching. He imagined signalling that there was an incoming attack, he imagined loading and firing the gun. The deafening sounds of war seemed almost incomprehensible in the near complete silence that now surrounded him. The smell of grease and gunfire had now been replaced with damp moss and sea air. He felt as though he was on the very edge of the world. What an amazing place. He closed his eyes.

The sound of his stomach rumpling brought Robbie back to the present and to the food in his rucksack. As he chomped on his chocolate, he watched the changing patterns of the clouds and the movement of the sea. Further out it seemed calm and brooding, darkness gathered, searching landward. Closer to shore, the waves lurched and surged, breaking over smaller, jutting rocks and smashing against the cliff base. On the retreat, the water swirled and spun as if trying to pull the land back with it, downward, into the abyss.

From where he stood, Robbie could see no sign of life within the water but the large mass seemed like a creature in itself. It was like a strange life form, trying to expand, to cling to the shore, only to lose grip and contract again. Creamy-white foam flared at the edges of the waves, rolling and spraying up, before being caught in the salty breeze and carried away. Dancing above the water, as if celebrating escape from the tide's clutches, the foam would soon dissolve into nothingness. Robbie could sometimes hear the thunderous power of water hitting rock, if the wind allowed it. Occasionally he caught a glimpse of a passing gannet or a still-unidentifiable gull, their calls carried, echoed and then lost somewhere on the cliff face below him. The rock that seemed so solid under his feet would eventually be eroded away by this monstrous liquid force. And so it had been for thousands of years, and so it would continue, with little care for artillery fire or dropping bombs.

Towards the horizon, Robbie watched a massive tanker cut its way through the distant waters as it made its slow journey to the Shetland oil terminal. To his left, he could see one end of a golden beach which looked deceptively warm and enticing. It was deserted. No-one, no dog-walker, no beachcomber, could brave the bracing sea breeze that whipped up the sand and rattled the shells. The ever-changing clouds seemed solid and plentiful. Some were white and bright and rounded, others formed layers of grey that hung heavy and damp, ready to replenish the sea and mist the faces of the tanker crew.

Some would say it was bleak; for Robbie it was invigorating. It lifted his spirit, filled his soul with clean air, carried away the dusty feelings of sadness that lay in him. It made him feel alive and, thankfully, insignificant. Nature, with its sheer cliffs and pounding waves, could leave you in no doubt that you were, in fact, not the centre of the universe. Was this just wilderness or was this proof of Mother Earth? Was this God? Robbie did not know. He just knew that he felt free.

The skin on Robbie's face tingled, as if slightly sun-burned or smeared with an astringent lotion. The wind and salt had acted as a spa treatment, stimulating his circulation and blushing his cheeks. He began to walk back towards the half-buried buildings. Their tops protruded like grassy pyramids. He made his way over woody tufts of heather and jumped down onto a perimeter pathway that led around one of the buildings like a concrete moat. This led through a rectangular opening and into a dark room. He switched on his torch. He could smell damp cement dust and stagnant water. Here, out of the wind, below ground level, there was an eerie stillness which brought with it a perceptible quiet. He heard water drip into a shallow puddle and echo into the space. Robbie was sure that if he stood still enough he would hear only the beating of his own heart and the scuttling of spiders. Around the entrance, rainwater trickled, and glistening algae seeped and oozed out towards the sunlight. Robbie felt fear, excitement and adrenaline.

He stepped inside and let his eyes adjust to the dim conditions. He followed the beam of his torch as he swept it left to right from ceiling to floor. Once the initial inspection was complete, Robbie's eyes had become more accustomed to the murky gloom. The cement room was not decorated and had not been used for many years, maybe decades. Sinister looking hooks hung on metal bars above rusty steel storage cupboards and a work surface. Some decayed wires and rocks were scattered about. On the opposite side, someone had upturned a small wooden rowing boat as if storing it in preparation for repair work to be done.

A small recess had once housed some shelves. A tiny window had been blacked-out for some time by fungi or mould. Below it lay the festering remains of a long-dead sheep carcass. Its rotting remnants no longer smelled pungent but there was a stale, musty odour around it. Robbie stepped back with fright as his ray of torchlight fell onto the exposed skull. The atmosphere felt thick and heavy; there was nothing more to see in here. He headed for the opening and stepped thankfully into the fresh air.

CHAPTER TEN

Robbie was spooked. He wanted so desperately to explore the other buildings, to unearth and discover, and answer all the questions that were running through his head. But it was too late, his imagination had complete control over all that was logical and rational. He threw his hands up above the cement wall that surrounded the path, grasping at the woody heather roots, tearing and ripping clumps of earth and stems as he rolled up to the perceived safety of the bank. He lay, wheezing, panting and staring into the brightening sky. It hurt to breathe with such intensity. When he closed his eyes, he could see negative images of the clouds. After a few minutes – long enough to feel a fool – Robbie accepted defeat for the day and reluctantly resigned himself to abandoning the mission.

He walked with heavy feet back to his bike at the bottom of the ski-jump track which, in this direction, promised an impossible upward assent. He held on to the handlebars and began to saunter. At the top of the track, where it met the marginally larger main road, he started to pedal southward, downhill, home. His mind and his wheels racing, Robbie knew only one thing for sure: he would do more research and then return. Information was power, and all that.

"I told you not to go alone, young man," Jack reiterated with a slight look of jokey satisfaction. "Although, in my opinion it is extremely beneficial to the formation of an inquisitive mind to be scared out of one's wits at regular intervals; it stops one rising above one's lowly station in life – stops you getting too big for your boots."

Robbie had no real idea what Jack was on about.

"Being frightened doesn't appeal to me – I can't see it having any short- or long-term benefits and it is not a feeling I want to repeat. And anyway, there was nothing to be frightened about – it's not as if I was under military attack. A dead sheep isn't exactly public enemy number one." Robbie was embarrassed. It was probably the most pathetic tale of cowardice the old man had heard in all his years.

"I can't judge. I once ran from an alleyway screaming in terror having mistaken my own shadow for an assailant in hot pursuit. It would have been a lot funnier to recount had I not been with a lady I was courting. Needless to say, I was not the 'man-of-the-moment', nor any subsequent moment. I never heard from her again," Jack kindly revealed. "Anyone with an imagination can have it run wild on occasion. I'd still rather have one."

"It's certainly an interesting place. The war was a difficult time and it is amazing to think that it changed even the landscape of a small island far removed from the main action. I am sure that, with such splendid panoramic views, the area would have also been used as a good defensive position for the ultimate northern warriors, much earlier settlers in Shetland."

"You mean in the First World War?" Robbie asked.

"No, no," Jack shook his head, "Vikings. They have left their mark here too – with remains being found all the time: longhouses, jewellery and weapons. They journeyed from Scandinavia over the North Sea in their longships – dragon headed row-boats with large sails and little comfort. They pillaged and fought their way southward like an unstoppable force. The Shetland place names and dialect are still greatly influenced by their conquering. Their legacy lives on in this culture and in Shetland myths and legends."

Robbie was fascinated. There had not been many tales of warriors in Harrow and Robbie had never been completely sure that Vikings had really existed until now. He pulled his computer out of his bag and went online.

"Let's Google some information," Robbie suggested. "I'd like to learn a bit more."

"I tell you what you should know about, if you live in Shetland," Jack began. "It's called Up Helly Aa, it's the annual Viking fire festival."

Robbie entered the name into the computer and clicked on 'images'. Jack was amazed, for within a few short seconds Robbie was flicking through photographs of men dressed in replica costumes, holding flaming torches, metal axes and shields. Pictures showed chain mail and winged helmets, fleece lined boots and velvet and leather cloaks. Jack talked him through the day.

"Each year, on the last Tuesday in January, the main town of Lerwick hosts the largest of many celebrations. Several groups, called squads, dress up – each with a different theme; they may be cartoon characters or political figures, creatures from mythology or television. The biggest Up Helly Aa is for men only, each man who dresses up is a guizer and the most important squad is the Jarl Squad. The Guizer Jarl is the head Viking, chosen years in advance, and his squad always dress as Vikings complete with axes and shields. It takes a year for them to make their costumes and for a life-sized replica longship to be built – this is the galley. The Jarl Squad pull the galley through the main town as thousands of people line the streets. The other squads follow behind, almost 1000 men in costume, all carrying flaming wooden torches. It is an amazing sight. The heat on the cold night and the smell of wood and tar, the orange glow; it's a spectacle. Music is played through speakers and special rousing songs are sung by the marchers. The galley is pulled towards the central park. The boat has been carefully carved and constructed from wood then painted and decorated, complete with oars and mast. All the guizers gather around with their flaming torches held high and, on the signal from the Guizer Jarl, they throw their torches into the boat and cheer as it burns to ash."

"Why do they do that? It seems a shame and a waste," Robbie commented.

"They are re-enacting the burial ritual of the Vikings when they would have put the body of an important warrior into his boat and set fire to it at sea, sending him to Valhalla – Viking heaven."

"Oh," Robbie seemed satisfied. "What happens then?"

"There are usually some fireworks. Then the guizers go around the town to different halls where the women are. They do short acts on stage and dance to traditional music, eat and drink and then move around to the next hall, until they have visited them all; this takes until about 7am. The Wednesday following Up Helly Aa is always a holiday in the main town. There is no school, nothing is open. During the rest of the year the Jarl Squad sometimes dress up for other special occasions, they visit schools and hospitals and any important visitors or ships that come to the islands. It is a real honour to be in the Jarl Squad and their outfits are kept and treasured."

"Have you ever been in the Jarl Squad?" Robbie asked.

"Not in Lerwick, no. But after that there is a different Up Helly Aa in many villages all around Shetland over the next few weeks. They don't all burn their boats, if they have one, and women can also be guizers. People dress up, march with torches, sing, act and dance. It helps to pass the time in the winter and gives everyone something to look forward to."

"It sounds amazing," said Robbie. "I'll be sure to tell mum about it and hopefully we can go and watch it next year."

"I think you should definitely make it part of your calendar."

"We can take you too," Robbie offered.

"Oh, I think I'll be in my own Valhalla by then," laughed Jack, only half joking.

"Aren't you scared of dying?" Robbie asked, rather suddenly.

"I've had a good life. It's going to happen; it's how it happens that most people are frightened of really. It's the fear of the unknown. What comes next? Will I be alone?"

Robbie searched for something outside the window, but answers were not to be found outside the windows of care homes. "Do you believe in God?"

"I do not believe that I am the reason the universe exists – no person is. I don't think any power of more consequence than humans would expect a human to understand it, just like I don't expect snails to understand me. Snails should focus on being good snails and we should focus on being good people, living good lives. I am not religious in any traditional sense," Jack summarised.

"What's a good life?" asked Robbie.

"We have to find that for ourselves. I don't think my good life is your good life. But love and kindness are something to do with all of us. That's as much as I could dare to say."

"Do you pray?"

"I'm not sure if I would call it that."

"Where do you think you will go when you die?"

"Baliasta Cemetery."

"I'm being serious."

"So am I."

Jack did not think he went anywhere that mere snailmen could comprehend.

"I am more motivated to live life to the full, with no regrets and to be a good person, knowing it will end. If it went on forever, there would be nothing to lose by hurting people and letting yourself get a little rough around the edges," he reiterated. "On my deathbed, I want to have a 'job well done' smile on my face."

"You want the church roof fixed though..."

"The church here is part of the community. It helps a lot of people. It has helped me, in its time. I wish I could find the peace and strength a lot of those members have. I don't believe religion is a bad thing; that's the fashion these days. I think people should be allowed to believe whatever helps them through the night."

"You talk about death a lot for a young person," he added.

The observation hung in the air without acknowledgment or rebuff.

Robbie wandered home. There were no sirens, no pizza places, no tearooms, no pound shops, no graffiti, no skate parks, no escalators, no galleries, no cinemas, no statues. But, he was not lonely, he was not bored, though it seemed likely he ought to be.

The fields were divided by fences and drystone walls, rather than hedges. Further up the hillside new born foals, the size of Labradors, nestled close to their Shetland pony mothers.

An oystercatcher flew by, low and straight. Its sharp call carried far into the distance. Robbie had phoned the retired vet to find out how his bird was doing and had been told it was making a very quick recovery and would be released soon. Robbie was pleased, even if it meant he would not be able to see it again. The sky was leaden, it would rain later.

Back at the Bed and Breakfast, Robbie switched on his computer to play some music. In Harrow he had spent half his evenings on this machine, disappearing into another world. It was escapism, a lie. A bit of a waste of time. He rarely played his computer games now – maybe he still would, if a friend came around. There was a boy in his class who seemed to like computers; more than people, maybe. Robbie was toying with the idea of asking him around some time. He knew this would reassure Ruth.

The last time he had been on the Internet, Robbie had done more research about Beth Wishart. He had found an address where she might be reached and had decided to write to her. Jack had advised using a pen, rather than a printer: "She'll appreciate that, I can tell," he had said. "It will stand out from all the other bills and letters."

Robbie pulled his writing pad closer to him. He told Ms. Wishart how he had acquired her book, how he had shown Jack the Internet and how often he used the reference book to help him as he tried to learn about the local wildlife. At the bottom he drew a cartoon oystercatcher. He would never, never have done this type of thing in Harrow, he thought.

CHAPTER ELEVEN

On Thursday evenings the doctor held a late surgery. It had been a while since Robbie had last seen Dr Hawkins so he had arranged with Ruth to give Robbie the last two appointments, allowing him extra time.

"It's nice to see you again," the doctor said on Robbie's arrival.

Ruth pulled a magazine off the waiting room table and settled herself.

Robbie walked into the familiar room. The clock. The sight test poster. The chair – offered to him by an outstretched, open hand.

The doctor looked tired. Maybe he had had a long day. Maybe someone was very unwell. He still managed to appear interested in all Robbie had to say (which Dr Hawkins hoped would be more than previous times).

"How are you sleeping?" he enquired, hoping that an open, but less abstract, question might gain a little insight.

"Maybe a bit better," offered Robbie. "Mum made me some darker curtains. But I don't want it to be completely dark."

The doctor considered pursuing this, but it was rather early in the session and he did not want to appear too pushy.

"Ruth tells me you've been decorating your room. Which colours did you decide on, in the end?"

Robbie looked a little brighter.

"It's black, white and orange. The curtains are black with a strip of orange and a strip of white ribbon going across near the bottom. The walls are mostly white and my bedding is black with an orange blanket and a pink cushion. I have pictures of birds framed in black and white. Mum helped me to do it, but I chose the colours. They are the colours of an oystercatcher, and I chose to use those because I found one and rescued it." It was the most he had ever said to the doctor in one go. Dr Hawkins wondered what would come next, if he just waited and smiled.

"Mum really liked my idea of using nature colours for rooms," he added. "She is going to redecorate the Bed and Breakfast accommodation over the winter, when it's quieter. Each room will be the colours of local birds and plants and flowers. She said I could choose them. I think it will look good. The doors will have little signs on them with the name of the room – I think 'Speedwell' will be one because mum really likes the white, yellow and indigo blue. And I would like one to be 'Wheatear'."

"Hmmmm," said the doctor. "Do your friends like the colours you've chosen?"

Robbie could see what the doctor was trying to do but he decided to answer.

"I don't know. I think I will ask Magnus over to play computer games soon. He's quite quiet. And I'll need to ask the guys I've met at Youth Club a couple of times." He glanced up, hoping to see an impressed look on the doctor's face. The doctor obliged.

"Do you find it easier to talk to your classmates? You were finding that a bit of a challenge last time."

"Well, Jack – you know, Jack from the care home, that I visit a lot? Jack has helped me to feel more confident to talk to people. I think that is why I can talk to adults, like you, better. But the kids in my class don't really like the same things I do. Not many of them notice the nature so much. They know about lambing and they know some species, but they don't read about it. I understand that though. They have grown up with it, it's normal to them. It would be like me living in Harrow and suddenly deciding to research pigeons, rats and foxes."

"What did you do at Youth Club?" the doctor asked.

"We had snacks and played five-a-side football. I was rubbish but no-one minded. Which is nice, I suppose."

"Have you played football before?"

"Not for ages. My dad used to take me to training at Harrow Recreation Ground, but it was a long time ago. I don't remember playing much, just running, going around cones and passing to each other a lot."

A silence hung in the air again. He knew what was coming next.

"Do you think about your dad much?"

That was a stupid question. Robbie looked at the doctor briefly and then at an anatomy poster.

"Have you told anyone what happened – Jack maybe?" the doctor asked, more persistently: he was ready to get to the nitty-gritty.

"No," Robbie replied. He sighed. "If I talk about it, it will be real again. Dad has gone. I know I won't see him again, but I think about him. I miss him."

"You probably know other people whose dads have left, but it is different for you," clarified the doctor.

"Some people's dads leave them and don't want to see them ever again; never call, write or contact them. I think that would be hard too," said Robbie. "My dad didn't leave me on purpose. He loved me. He didn't want to die."

And that was the start of it. The words came. Tumbling out.

How he could still remember seeing his father, lying unconscious. The smell of the room. The sound of the respirator. It was so unusual to see his dad motionless, because Robbie remembered him being such an active man, always on the move. The doctors carrying out their tests. His dad being unresponsive. Intermittent flurries of activity from the staff then periods of quiet contemplation. At other beds around the wards other families had their own crises, as if in their own opaque trauma bubble. It was intense. Adults were crying. Strangely, Robbie could vividly recall every vein, every odour, the dry Ploughman's Sandwich, the feel of his father's limp fingers. He had whispered into his father's ear; told him he loved him. Told him, he always would. His father had never regained consciousness. Never spoken again. Robbie had tried to come to terms with the fact that he would never see him smile, never have his encouragement and support whenever he tried something new or brought him a new idea or creation. His dad would never be able to talk to him about girls or show him how to shave. Never pretend to gang up with him against Ruth when they wanted to watch sport on TV. He would never pick him up from his friend's house or help him with his exams. He would never wake Robbie up by singing out of tune before work or steal Robbie's chips or tell him when he was being out of line. His father would never again embarrass him at the school gates or clap too loud at an end of term performance. He was gone. The man on that bed was not his dad. His dad was gone. Robbie had felt utterly helpless. The whole situation seemed futile and such a waste of life and potential.

Robbie carried on. Telling Dr Hawkins how Ruth had been inconsolable but tried to hide it from Robbie. She had not been able to function for a few weeks and her mother, Robbie's grandmother, had moved in with them. Granny Jackson had helped organise the funeral and helped around the house, but what Ruth really needed was time and some grief counselling. Robbie felt that no-one had really noticed that Robbie was spiralling downward and disappearing inside himself. They were looking out for trouble; bad behaviour, fights, anger. When it did not come, they believed he was maybe coping quite well. But actually, he felt he was slowly, but completely, engulfed in a depression, a despair, a decline. He understood why Ruth was not able to give anything emotionally to anyone else. He watched as she got over her own incapacity, cut off her feelings and became almost robotic. She had busied herself and become very factual and precise. She had begun to plan the move and the starting-again. Everyone copes with grief and trauma in a different way. Nothing is wrong, nothing is predictable. Robbie had not been sure if it was the right thing to be moving from his school and his friends, but he said nothing and was thankful to be out of their house; out the house full of memories of life and death.

Granny Jackson had moved back to her house. She phoned often but Ruth had wanted to get settled before inviting her to visit Unst. Ruth did not want to rely on her mother too much. She wanted to make a success of the business and make sure Robbie got the help he now obviously needed. Outside help. Ruth knew she couldn't manage it herself. She was sad, but not depressed; there was a difference. Robbie, once unreachable, was slowly surfacing again; rebuilding, recovering, re-emerging. Ruth was so thankful that the new freedom and community had embraced Robbie and cocooned him when he needed it most. Her husband would have been proud of her. Somewhere, he was proud of her, still.

The room was quiet again. Robbie had talked. A lot. He had spoken about his dad out loud. He had told someone. He was not crazy, he was not angry, he was just a boy who had become overwhelmed.

⚓ ⚓ ⚓

When Robbie eventually told Jack that his dad had died, Jack said "yes, I know."

"How did you know?" Robbie had asked him.

"I just knew," Jack had said. And then, "they say there are two types of people; those who have already lost a parent and those who have not. You will never be the same again but you are a better person for having known such a good man. You will always have memories of him; you will know what he would have said and done in different situations."

Robbie wondered who 'they' were. 'They say...' Maybe this time 'they' were right. There did seem to be a void between him and the other children; an invisible barrier, a lack of connection. Something about Robbie felt more adult than it should be at his age. He was not as happy-go-lucky as the other kids; he worried about mortality, they worried about which phone to buy. He worried about getting a good job so he could help support his mother; they worried about what deodorant to use to impress the girls. He knew some of his classmates thought he was aloof but at least they did not bother him and he, in turn, did not bother them. Had they all been in a bigger class, no-one would have noticed or cared. He had wanted to be known as 'Robbie' and not 'The Boy Whose Dad Died'. He had not wanted pity, attention or sympathy; he just wanted to be left alone until he was ready. Now, having spoken to the doctor and Jack about it, he had found that talking did help release what had been bottled up inside. He had enjoyed telling Jack about all the happy memories of time spent with his father, his funny mannerisms and idiosyncrasies. It was not fair on Ruth, or his father, to let people continue to assume his dad left them and did not bother to even visit, to assume that they got divorced when they had actually been very happy.

Robbie was coming to realise that everyone has 'something' – something that has happened to them; baggage, history, a bad experience, something hidden inside. The more choices people make, the more chance there is of some of those choices being wrong. The more friends people meet, the more chance there is that some of those friends will disappoint. Robbie's father's death had impacted him, not just because he had lost a loved one, an irreplaceable parent. He had had to come to terms with injustice, the anger and disillusionment brought about by a troubling realisation – that bad things happened to good people, a very difficult lesson to learn.

CHAPTER TWELVE

"My Uncle Charlie told me on the phone that he knows you," she said.

"I don't really know anyone here," Robbie told her.

"He doesn't live here," she said.

"Does he live in Harrow?" Robbie asked.

"Where? No," she said. "He lives in Stonehaven."

"I don't know anyone in Stonehaven," said Robbie, "I've never been there."

Robbie did not understand girls. He wanted to, and he did like them, but he did not understand the way they said things in a round-about kind of way. His brain often hurt when he talked to one. There was often lots of drama and elaborating and very detailed re-telling. Robbie learned quickly that some girls could remember very casual conversations in minute detail, as if they were specifically important or going to be used later as part of a crime investigation. That level of detail, told and re-told, although it seemed completely inconsequential. Life would be so much simpler if, like the birds, he just had a bright plumage. Having said that, he was glad he did not have to sing to impress the girls.

With boys it was simpler – if you didn't get on there was an understanding to stay out of each other's way. Later in life they may go through a phase of fighting or being competitive but, at the moment, that was way too much effort. But girls that Robbie did not like were really, really annoying. Their voices carried, like high-pitched squawking, over huge distances. They always told stories as though they were funny or very interesting, but they were not. The girls Robbie did like (which was most of them), he really liked. He thought about them, his palms got sweaty when they spoke to him and he could never think what to say.

"Charlie Hughson. That's his name. He stayed at your Bed and Breakfast," she said. At last – concrete information of some practical use when communicating with another human being.

"Oh. Yes. Charlie. Yes, I met him. He was very nice. He helped me heal an injured bird and get it released back into the wild. How is Charlie doing?" Robbie said.

"He's ok," she said. "He said to tell you 'hi'. He is coming up again in September to look for migrant birds."

"Is he? Do you know anything about migrant birds?" Robbie asked her.

"No," she said, confused. "He just told me to tell you, that's all." Robbie was a little disappointed. He had hoped she would be more interested and that they could have sat near the school pond and bird watched at break times.

'She' was Megan. A classmate. A girl he happened to like.

"Megan, would you like to know about migrant birds before your Uncle comes back to visit? If you do, let me know. I like nature." Robbie surprised himself by being so confident.

"We know you like nature," she laughed. "It's all you ever write stories about or draw in class. Maybe. Uncle Charlie would like that. Maybe," she said again, in a girlie, non-committal, ambiguous kind of way. Robbie was not sure what to say after that. He had been pretty clear in offering her some help, so the ball was in her court. He was quite sure he was not going to see the ball again. Ever.

🐦🐦🐦

In his spare time, Robbie continued to work on his collecting and cataloguing. His scrapbooks were full of feathers, which he had carefully annotated after researching which birds they may have come from. For some of them, he even managed to discover which part of the bird they were from.

He had glued in some flowers but, over time, they dried to a dull brown colour or went mouldy and black. Robbie had printed some of his photographs during a visit to the town – he had a star fish, seal and beached jellyfish. He had also added some pictures from magazines and sketches he had done outside. In a bowl on his desk he had put his serpentine along with other nice rocks, shells and broken bits of pottery which he had found when digging the garden. He had recently added a large orangey-red crab claw and a jagged piece of a spiny sea urchin too.

At the Youth Club one evening, Robbie decided to ask Magnus if he wanted to visit the Bed and Breakfast. Magnus had accepted. When the day came, Robbie had become a little nervous; he was not sure why. He did not fear Magnus's opinions or judgements, in fact, he felt sure the quiet boy would not voice any. He may, however, ask questions.

Ruth was very pleased that Robbie was starting to do things which were more typical of a boy his age. She had met Magnus's mother at the shop and thought she was positive and vivacious, quite different to Robbie's description of her son.

"Hi," said Magnus, upon his arrival at the porch door where Robbie greeted him.

"My mum said because it was my first visit and I am staying for food, I had to give your mum this," he said, and he handed Robbie a box of chocolates.

"Mum is in the kitchen," Robbie informed him. "I think you should tell her that yourself. Come through." He led Magnus through the hall and towards the delicious smells.

"Hello Mrs Alderson. These chocolates are from my mum. And me. To say thanks. For having me. And for dinner," Magnus managed to say.

"Hi Magnus." Robbie's mum wiped her hands on the tea towel that was slung over her shoulder. She shook Magnus's surprised hand and said "Please, call me Ruth." She knew Magnus probably wouldn't.

After a few computer games, some biscuits and juice and a bit of TV, it turned out that Magnus was not as shy as Robbie had thought. If he was not in a large crowd, or talking to an adult, he was quite funny and interesting. Magnus enjoyed racing games more than shooting games on the computer. He had never been abroad but made and collected model cars and wanted to start doing weights (but his mum wouldn't let him yet). His ambitions were to watch a Formula One Grand Prix in real life and to learn how to play the guitar. He loved pie and chips but hated mushrooms. He was a bit scared of flying but he had been rod fishing in the bay in his dad's boat. He said he would ask his dad if Robbie could come with them next time.

Robbie told Magnus all about his love of nature – although it was pretty self-evident. They talked about Jack, the differences between Harrow and Unst and what it is like to live in a Bed and Breakfast.

They were very hungry by the time Ruth called them for dinner – beef stew and herb dumplings with creamy mashed potatoes and green beans. For dessert she had made apple and sultana crumble with extra oats and nuts in the topping and vanilla custard. They drank banana milkshake that Ruth made with real fruit. Magnus was in his own little food Valhalla – one happy customer.

After they had finished, they could barely move so they crashed in front of the TV and flicked through channels in the way no adult understands. Magnus rubbed his belly and tried not to laugh, but they laughed quite a lot, at nothing in particular.

Ruth suggested they went for a walk so, with nature books in hand, they wandered passed the Post Office and down to the shoreline. While they were there they tried to skim stones, with limited success, and turned rocks over to watch various small insecty-creatures darting for cover, being careful not to kill anything. Sometimes they would try to sketch. Robbie heard a familiar call and looked up.

"It's only a shalder," Magnus said, without lifting his gaze off a limpit.

"No, it's an oystercatcher," Robbie corrected him. He'd never heard of a shalder; he had never seen it mentioned in his books. He wondered if this bird was the one he had saved.

"A shalder is an oystercatcher," Magnus said, casually. "It is the Shetland name for one."

'The Shetland name for one'. Robbie had known there were Shetland words – unique words used in Shetland dialect. These were the words that made it almost impossible for a visitor to understand what was being said by two chatting locals. He knew that Shetlanders modified their speech so that newcomers could understand them, this was called 'knappin'. Robbie had now learned some Shetland words himself: 'peerie' (little, like Jack's peerie cup), 'dastreen' (yesterday), 'brawly' (very/quite), 'yundrew' (there).

Jack used Shetland words sometimes, when he was relaxed and forgot to knap. He had never mentioned that there were Shetland words for most of the birds, as well as many other creatures and plants. This was a revelation to Robbie and he wanted to learn as many of the words as he could.

"Do you know the Shetland names?" he asked Magnus.

"Most of them. I think so. I'm sometimes not sure of the proper names though..." Magnus confessed.

Robbie got his nature notebook and began to scribble furiously. In one column he listed all the birds he could think of. At the top he wrote 'Common name' (he didn't know the Latin or Scientific names for any birds yet). In the other column he wrote 'Shetland name'. He then got his nature book out to point to pictures of the birds that Magnus wasn't sure about.

"Puffin?"

"Tammie Norie."

"Tammie Norie? I love that name!" said Robbie and resolved to call puffins 'Tammie Nories' from now on.

"Fulmar?"

"Not sure," Magnus looked at the book. "Oh, Maalie. Those things are so disgusting. Do you know they will throw up this oily, stinky stuff all over you if you go too close to their nests? You can never get the smell out, no matter how often you wash your clothes, so you just have to throw them away," he added, rather dramatically. He wrinkled his face up at the malodorous memory.

Robbie pondered this new information for a moment: 'note to self', he thought, '(i) don't go bird watching in good clothes and (ii) learn where fulmars typically nest so you don't get vommed on, inadvertently.'

"Arctic Skua?"

"Skootie Alan," Magnus raised both his eyebrows, as if to say 'can you believe it?'

"Great Skua?"

"Bonxie."

"Are you joking me? Bonxie? These are fantastic. It's like learning code words for everything!" Robbie laughed. "What about Arctic Tern?" He tapped his book at the correct illustration.

"Tirrick."

Robbie wrote it down.

Magnus confessed he couldn't remember any more names but would check with his granddad and let Robbie know of any more.

Robbie loved learning and Magnus loved feeling interesting and clever.

As they neared the Bed and Breakfast, Magnus noticed the shed.

"What's in there?" he asked.

"Not much, mum puts stuff in the garage. I thought about using this as a henhouse, if she lets me."

"Can we go in?" asked Magnus.

The boys spent the last hour of Magnus's visit clearing out the ramshackle shed. First they took out the rubbish, then swept it. Robbie tried to patch up a couple of holes with his tool kit and wooden off-cuts. He opened up two folding fishing chairs and brought in an old stool and a chest of drawers which Ruth kept meaning to take to the skip near the pier. In the garage Robbie found some white gloss and a brush and the boys took turns painting the stool and the chest.

"We can examine our nature finds here," said Robbie, as Magnus wiped the window clean of mud and cobwebs. "It will be our research workshop. I'll add the things we need.

"I'll see what I can find at home too," said Magnus, eagerly. Both boys agreed they had really enjoyed their evening.

"Thank you for dinner Mrs... Ruth," Magnus called through to the kitchen before leaving.

"Thanks for the chocolates Magnus. Come and visit any time," Ruth called back as she emptied yet another load from the washing machine.

Before Magnus had arrived back home there was a new sign on Robbie's bedroom door. It read 'Welcome to Shalder'.

CHAPTER THIRTEEN

School was more interesting than Robbie remembered it being in Harrow. This was partly because there were fewer kids in his class, but also because lessons were not disrupted by bad behaviour. He sometimes missed the cultural diversity of the London Borough, but Unst had its own advantages.

Miraculously, school lunches were varied and delicious. The pond had become a buzzing mass of life and the vegetable plot was tended and fertilized, ensuring a bumper crop appeared almost ready for harvesting. His class had enjoyed a day trip to Lerwick where they had visited the Up Helly Aa museum and the historical archives. Rehearsals had begun for the end of year performance. There were lunchtime and after school clubs in full swing and sports day was fast approaching. Staying busy had helped Robbie sleep better; he had less time to over-analyse what had come before. He now appreciated the present and looked forward to the future with more positivity.

For the first time he had become friends with people of different ages. Jack had been right when he said learning would become easier because Robbie was training his brain to concentrate and research, even if he wasn't engaged in a topic at the outset.

History, however, was still a mental block for Robbie. Jack made it appealing and relevant but, within the confines of the school curriculum, it often seemed too prescribed and dry. During a more stimulating lesson, Robbie was paired with Megan. Their task was to do some Shetland-based research and make a presentation to the class the following week. Megan knew she had more expertise in these matters than Robbie and she revelled in her opportunity to take the dominant role.

Magnus and Stuart had already presented a funny and fascinating account of the 'Herring Boom', when the fishing industry was at its height between 1880 and 1925. They had worn a variety of cardboard masks and spoken in funny voices. First they were fishermen, describing the conditions and methods used to land a successful catch from 'Da Far Aaf' fishing ground. Then they were 'fisher wives', the women who worked tirelessly at the pier, gutting and preparing the fish. This had been met with hoots of laughter from the class. The duo had set a high standard for the assignment.

"What could we talk about?" Robbie asked Megan. They had pushed two desks together at the back of the class and were staring at a flashing cursor on the computer screen.

"I don't think we should try to be funny, like the boys," she conceded. "If we choose the right topic then we should be able to get people's attention. Maybe we could do a PowerPoint on the interactive white board and then have a couple of props, just to keep the momentum."

Robbie began to wish he'd been in Magnus's group.

"Well, what could we talk about?" he asked again.

They flicked through a couple of reference books that the teacher had put on their desk. Eventually Megan made a decision.

"I think we should talk about the St Ninian's Isle Treasure," she declared. Robbie had never heard of it. And Megan knew that Robbie probably wouldn't have heard of it. He waited for her to elaborate. It did sound quite interesting, he admitted to himself.

"What would you like to know?" Megan asked him. "Whatever it is, that is what we have to put in our presentation. Write down your first questions here." She pushed a notepad in Robbie's direction and began looking on the Internet. "Tell me what you're writing and I'll see how fast I can find the answer. You can write the answers next to your questions, then we'll make them into a slideshow." Robbie was acutely aware that he had been given the least fun role but he recognised that Megan had come up with a logical strategy for getting started.

"Um. I think we should start with who, what, where, when, why, how questions. Who found it? What did they find? Where was it?" he suggested.

"Those are the questions, I suppose," said Megan, "but we can't answer them in that order. First we would have to show a map and say where and when it all happened."

Robbie could tell Megan was going to become a teacher. He nodded at her.

"Then we'd have to say who was there and what they were doing and then what they found and why it is important. Is there anything else you would like to know?" she asked Robbie.

"I'd like to know where it is now and how much it is worth and how they know it is real. And if there is any more treasure anywhere," he responded.

"Good. Good. Write all that down," Megan commanded, and she began to look for a suitable map and dates online.

Megan and Robbie had to work on their presentation for homework during the week. They spent their lunch breaks in the history room deciding who would say what and practising their lines. Robbie made replica treasure at home using cardboard and tinfoil and collected a couple of other props from around the Bed and Breakfast. As the lesson approached, they both got quite nervous.

"Megan and Robbie, can you come and set up?" Mrs Boyle asked, as they entered the class on the big day. Megan connected the computer and Robbie hid his items under the desk. He took a couple of deep breaths. At the same time Mrs Boyle collected homework and asked the rest of the class what they could remember about the Herring Fishing.

She looked over at Megan and nodded. It was time. Robbie spoke first.

"Welcome to our presentation," he opened. "Now, like a lot of people, I sometimes like digging in my garden to see what I can discover." He put his hands under the desk in preparation. "So far, all I have found are a few bits of broken pottery..." He held up a large piece of ceramic plate. "I also found lots of these..." Robbie's other hand appeared clutching a handful of live worms he had brought to school in a plastic container.

"Eugh!" laughed the class. He had their attention.

"Just imagine if, one day, you went exploring and you found something amazing, something important, something worth a fortune..." Cue Megan.

"Well, that's exactly what happened to Douglas Coutts in 1958. The school boy was digging at St Ninian's Isle when he found treasure – 28 objects all buried in a box made of larch wood."

Robbie stood next to the map that appeared on the screen. He pointed to St Ninian's Isle with one of his mother's knitting needles.

"Thank you for getting us up to speed Megan. But I think our audience may have more questions. They might be thinking: How did they know the treasure was real and what was it made from?"

"They had expert opinions and tests which have shown it was Pictish, from 800AD, and it was all made of silver," Megan responded.

"OK. How much did he sell it for?" Robbie asked.

"Well, it was donated to a museum."

"Lastly, Where is the treasure now?"

"It can be found in the National Museum of Scotland, in Edinburgh. It is free to go and look at it, although you can't touch any of the bowls, pins and other objects because they are behind glass."

"Are you sure about that Megan?" Robbie asked dramatically as he placed his tinfoil replicas onto the desk.

Megan pretended to look shocked. They both gave a small bow.

Everyone laughed and clapped and began talking about the presentation. Mrs Boyle looked impressed.

"Excellent work," she congratulated them. "But I will deduct points if those worms aren't immediately removed from my desk and put into the school compost heap," she added.

*   *   *

"How did it go?" asked Ruth as soon as Robbie got home.

"Really well, I think," he told her. "People laughed and looked amazed. Megan did a good job too."

He told his mum all about it as they had some of his favourite chocolate fudge cake.

"One day I'm going to buy a metal detector," he told her. Ruth had no doubt that one day, he probably would.

After dinner Robbie went behind the house with the spade. He was inspired to do some more digging.

It had rained a little. The soil smelled fresh and earthy. He didn't find much. For a while he just listened to his iPod and thought about nothing.

There were times when Robbie needed a physical challenge, he was becoming more like his dad in this way. He wasn't traditionally 'sporty' but now he couldn't sit still for long. He still walked a lot, and now went further up into the hills. He had watched peat being cut and dried ready to fuel the open fires of cottages in the winter time. Robbie knew his friends in Harrow would hardly recognise him; taller, broader, calmer. He was more focussed and happier to be himself.

As the days passed, every verge was speckled with tiny, exotic looking marsh orchids, speedwell and self-heal. Into the longer, damp grass sprouted lady's smock and red campion. Fiery bird's foot trefoil and cruelly-named milkwort dotted the road side. Year-on-year these hardy blooms triumphed over the passing exhaust fumes, the hungry rabbits and the brutal winter's bitter frost. Closer to the beach, sea pinks turned their papery petals towards what little sunshine there was.

The shed was a work in progress. Magnus came over most weeks and Ruth had been supportive of the makeover. Even though it was her busy season, she had taken Robbie to the skip at the pier. There they had found a little table. Robbie had set up a row of empty coffee jars to store some of his findings. He labelled them; shells, stones, feathers. Magnus donated an old fish tank. The pump had broken and his fish had not survived long but the boys let it fill with rain water and then added algae and beetles from the pond. They tried to keep count, but it was almost impossible. Ruth gave them a couple of house plants, a framed picture of Muckle Flugga lighthouse and some postcards of local wildlife. Robbie bought a magnifying glass in Lerwick one weekend and moved his paints and wind-up radio into the shed too. Pride of place, hanging on a nail on the end wall, was a large ram's skull. Robbie had found it in a field, complete with curly horns. It reminded him of the dead sheep he had encountered at Lambaness, when the carcass had frightened him away from the dilapidated site. He was now determined to revisit and further explore the strange location but, this time, he would not go alone.

CHAPTER FOURTEEN

There were almost no trees on Unst so monitoring the changing seasons was harder than in other areas – the clues had to come from flowers and animals. It was more-often-than-not overcast and breezy. Sea breezy.

Time went by with the seasons. Robbie and Megan spent more time together and, as the summer holidays approached, they were often joined by her older brother, James. Together they went guddling in the peaty burns, pond dipping and in search of the elusive and unique Edmonston's Chickweed flower, although it was still too early. Many hours were spent drawing, talking and observing in the shed.

Interesting visitors arrived and departed from the Bed and Breakfast; they came from all over the world to explore the islands and enjoy the relative peace and quiet. Robbie often spoke with them and the trio put a world map on the shed wall to mark where the guests had come from. Most arrived via the overnight boat from Aberdeen or on a short flight to Sumburgh Airport. Sometimes, tourists came to Unst by yacht and moored their vessels near the pier.

One clear evening, a cool breeze refreshed the children during a wander to the shoreline. A peachy light edged over the hillside and cast navy blue shadows around the old cottage ruins and drystone walls of the neighbouring fields. Sea birds' calls carried across the water as it lapped gently over rounded pebbles and glistening seaweed. The children sat on larger rocks that provided a good vantage point over the beach and to the distant horizon. Often the children were quiet. There were many times on Unst when there was no pressure to do or to say anything in particular. James threw shingle into water below.

"What shall we do at the weekend?" asked the older boy. He was only the class above Megan and Robbie but stood a full ten centimetres taller. "Do you want to try looking for otters again? Mr Cluness says there are some near the ferry terminal. There are always fish around there too. That would be a long cycle but we could take a picnic."

"I don't feel like that," said Megan. "I'd rather do something a bit more exciting."

"There's nothing more exciting than seeing otters in the wild, I don't think," James said, rather indignantly.

"I know what we can do," offered Robbie, hoping to keep the peace. "Why don't we go to Lambaness? I told you about the last time I went there so it would probably be best for me to have company this time! And besides, you said you haven't been there for years and can hardly remember it. Do you dare to join me?" he laughed.

James looked at Megan. She raised her eyebrows and tilted her head to the side, then she looked at her brother and nodded once, slowly.

"Ok," said James. "We'll ask Mum. Hopefully we can spend all day on Saturday. I have a geography project to do on Sunday after football practice. We'll bring crisps and sausage rolls, can you bring drinks and sandwiches?"

James could be even more bossy and organised than his sister. Although it was sometimes annoying, it was probably a good thing overall; there would be nothing worse than getting hungry in the middle of an adventurous and energetic day out. There were no fast food restaurants or handy corner shops on Unst where they could purchase supplies.

"I'll see what I can do," promised Robbie.

Although Ruth was busy she always tried to find time in the day to hear Robbie's plans and marvel at his sightings and discoveries. Her late husband would have delighted in their son's maturing and caring attitude and his interest in all that was around him. Ruth was proud of Robbie and loved engaging him in discussions and debates, always while attending to some other task. As she ironed, she heard all about his plans to revisit Lambaness. Of course there would be sandwiches and juice. Of course there would be home-baked cookies and muffins. Ruth assured Robbie that, if he did all his homework on Friday night, she would provide a bag of tasty treats on Saturday morning. Robbie didn't argue; he liked getting his work out the way so that the weekend was free – just in case the weather was fine.

When the day came, Ruth was busy serving bacon, eggs, beans and sausages to Hans and Myrtle from Austria. True to her word, a small rucksack of carefully packed plastic tubs and labelled zip-lock bags was waiting for Robbie on a kitchen chair. He had completed his maths and literacy homework the previous evening, accompanied by the smell of fresh chocolate chip cookies. Cherry muffins had sat on the cooling rack, tempting him. There were surely few finer distractions to studies than the aroma of food made with love and the promise of an exciting day with friends.

James and Megan cycled up to the Bed and Breakfast just after nine. The journey was expected to take almost two hours each way so they set off immediately in single file.

The first stretch of road was straight and level, taking them up to 'Bobby's Bus Shelter' – a local attraction unexpectedly filled with home comforts, stylish and topical decoration and working electrics. A sharp turn to the left led past the Keen of Hamar nature reserve to the garage and renewable energy centre. Here the children could see two small wind turbines slowly spinning, indicating that there was not much wind today. This made for an easier cycle up and around Nikka Vord Hill. All was quiet in the quarry on their left as they freewheeled down the steep hill into Haroldswick. A life-sized replica Viking longship stood at the point where the road levelled again and a couple of tourists were taking photographs of it.

The sea in the bay was a deep blue. Cream and light grey houses dotted the fields that hugged the coast. Purple spikes of spotted orchids poked through the marsh grasses. A winding road led through the small village and up to Saxa Vord, the former RAF base where boxy one-storey buildings and rusting metal fences still gave it an institutional quality. Newer houses, deeper inside the complex, had been converted into a holiday facility and restaurant but Robbie still felt there was something soulless and utilitarian about the area.

Overhead, the whirring sound of displaying snipe reverberated. Jack had told Robbie that this sound, so typical of Shetland, was produced by the snipe's tail feathers vibrating as they dived through the air.

The children were thankful to stop off at Norwick beach for some refreshments. They climbed onto the grassy area that rose up from the sands and looked out to sea as they enjoyed juice and a muffin.

"I loved the downhill. I don't think I've ever been so fast on a bike," exclaimed Megan. Her cheeks were flushed and her hair windswept where it had been forced to curl up around her helmet.

"You won't love it so much on the way home..." her brother pointed out. Crumbs circled the perimeter of his mouth and his freckles gave him a healthy, outdoors look.

Robbie watched as a couple of gannets expertly folded their wings and dropped, like missiles, into the waves. He should have taken his binoculars. They could see the cliffs that wrapped themselves around Lambaness; sheer and foreboding.

The three climbed back down to the beach, over limpets and mussels that hung to the barnacle-clad rocks. The tide was coming in towards the beach grass on the dunes. Their trio of bikes lay untouched at the end of the road, ready to ascend the final track towards Lambaness. The original Skaw road, which led to Britain's most northerly hamlet, was now closed and precarious. Erosion had resulted in crumbling sections falling into the sea below. A new access to the north had been created. It was steep – a precipitous climb that the children were unable to conquer on their bikes. They pushed their handlebars slowly upward, the view being the only immediate reward for their considerable efforts.

At the summit they sat on a roadside verge, cushioned by a carpet of wildflowers and springy moss. Never had lemonade tasted so thirst-quenching, never had crisps seemed so nourishing. James lay back and looked into the adjacent field of docken leaves and buttercups. A slight heat haze blurred the distant fence posts and lifted the smell of new tarmac into the air. For a few moments the children dozed, listening only to the sound of nearby insects and the bleating of sheep. Infrequently, a small puff of cloud would obscure the sun for a brief instant and blanket the children under a cool shadow. They were nearly at their destination but Robbie was too content to feel any apprehension about what else might be lurking in the bowels of the strange buildings.

The final push was not as difficult as their rested legs had anticipated. The flat single track led through a vast expanse of heathery moorland, uninterrupted by buildings or traffic and the children soon turned right onto the ski-jump road to the heart of Lambaness. They proceeded with their fingers firmly around their brake levers.

"I really don't remember being here with Mum," said Megan.

"I can," confirmed James, "but not clearly. I don't think we actually went in to the buildings last time. Isn't it amazing how they are hidden so effectively?"

The children put down their bikes and helmets and continued on foot. Initially they were all happy to wander around, observing the structures from different angles, chatting about what it might have been like in the war and what they could turn the buildings into if they had lots of money.

"One could be a cinema!" Megan decided, excitedly.

"I think they would make an amazing restaurant and hotel," Robbie added.

Eventually the children were ready to go inside. They chose one of the largest pyramids; one Robbie had not yet been into. Daisies and thistles grew around it. The concrete path circling the entrance was a couple of metres down from the edge where the children now lay on their stomachs. On the other side the access was a little easier so they decided to lower themselves there and walk around the slimy path to the opening. They helped each other and were soon looking into the dark doorway. Robbie could smell the familiar odour of mildew and damp cement. Rainwater percolated through the door frame and dripped periodically into small puddles beneath. Megan went in first.

With the help of torches, the children could see most of the interior was one large room, with a high ceiling and unexpectedly vertical walls. The space was practically empty except for some discarded wooden pallets, an old tyre and a coil of fencing wire.

"No dead sheep in here, by the looks of things," teased James, his voice echoing slightly against the enclosed space.

"Very funny," said Robbie. "With these acoustics maybe we should turn this place into a recording studio," he added, trying to change the subject.

Without warning James moved towards a small side door that led around a corner at the far end of the larger room and disappeared from view. Almost immediately there followed the sound of debris falling and a loud, prolonged shout of pure pain. Megan and Robbie looked at each other and ran to the second doorway. Inside there was a deep concrete-lined pit which now contained some wooden fencing posts held together with barbed wire, and James. He was crying and wincing in pain and clutching at his leg. His cheek was bleeding where it had scratched against some of the wire he had tripped on but he was lucky not to have knocked himself unconscious.

"James! Are you ok?" asked Megan, predictably. "Can you get out?"

James tried to catch his breath. He whimpered and held himself.

"No. No. My leg. It's broken, I'm sure," he whispered. He had heard it crack as he landed and then the fence posts had been pulled down on top of him. He was huddled in a corner, half covered, unable to move.

"What do we do? What do we do?" Megan panicked. She turned to Robbie for answers.

He looked at his phone. There was no signal.

CHAPTER FIFTEEN

Robbie and Megan stared down at James in disbelief. Megan was upset; someone had to decide what to do.

Robbie felt surprisingly clear and composed. "James, you need to answer some questions so that we can get the right help. Did you bump your head, do you think?"

"No, I don't think so," James answered.

"Can you feel your arms and legs? Do you think you're cut?"

"I don't think I'm cut except on my face. I can move my hands and feet but I can't feel my legs properly or move them because of the fence posts on them. I know I should feel a lot of pain, maybe my body is in shock."

"There's nothing we can do ourselves, James. I'm going to have to try and get some help, do you agree?"

"Yes," said James.

Robbie told Megan to sit and talk to James to keep him conscious and calm. She passed him down some water and her jacket to keep himself warm.

Robbie was not sure what to do as he scrambled out of the building and up the path, up into the open. There was still no mobile phone signal. He looked around, it was probably 300 metres to the end of the road and hardly any cars would pass by in the course of a day. In the hope that the higher ground might give him phone reception, Robbie clambered up the side of the grassy mound to the top of the buried building. Once there he held up his phone and hoped he would be able to connect a call. The words 'Emergency Calls Only' appeared on the screen. Robbie dialled 999.

When prompted, he asked for an ambulance. When he was put through, he told the lady on the line his unusual circumstances and the location of the fall. She tried to keep him calm and collect as much information from him as she could. She seemed impressed that he knew so much about the casualty's condition. Robbie could hear her tap on a keyboard.

"We're really in the middle of nowhere," he reiterated. There was a short pause.

"Robbie, the coastguard helicopter has been carrying out a practise exercise relatively close to your location. The crew has agreed to attend to James and will arrive far quicker than the air ambulance could. You will have to stay visible so the pilot can land as close as he can."

"Ok", Robbie said.

"Do you need me to call anyone for you?" the lady asked him.

Relief spread through Robbie's body as he asked the lady to call Ruth and contact Megan and James' parents. After the phone call ended, he shouted down to Megan and she appeared in the doorway.

"Help is coming. Tell James there will be people here soon," Robbie told her. She smiled a little and disappeared to tell her brother the news.

Less than ten minutes later Robbie could hear the sound of rotors cutting through the quiet. The familiar red and white body of the coastguard helicopter appeared over the cliffs to the south and sped effortlessly in his direction. Robbie waved his hands frantically in a large sweeping gesture above his head. The aircraft decelerated to a hover. It was close enough for Robbie to feel the turbulence it created. He decided to move down and shelter behind the mound of the building, as the crew had clearly seen him. Within a few seconds the blades of the helicopter were slowing, the red nose of the cockpit facing Robbie's direction. A minute later two men in orange flying suits were running towards the accident site, one carrying a case.

"He's down here," Robbie pointed. "Thank you for coming so quickly," he added.

The two men jumped down onto the path and into the area where James lay injured. They spoke with both siblings to ascertain the current situation. Very slowly, they began removing the fencing which had both tripped and trapped the boy. With the help of a powerful torch, the men – introduced as Ben and Alan – worked steadily until James could be examined.

"Megan, you've done a great job keeping your brother informed of what has been going on," said Alan. "James, we need to get you looked at and then we shall attach you to a stretcher to move you to the helicopter. We are hoping to take you to the Lerwick hospital within the next hour or so."

Another man, Geoff, arrived carrying a stretcher.

"Your parents are on their way and will accompany you to hospital," he told James.

"It certainly seems as though you have a leg fracture above the ankle," said Ben. "The good news is everything else seems intact, although you'll probably have some bruising."

Robbie stayed with James and the men as they carefully brought him out of the pit and laid him onto the stretcher. Straps were used to secure him. Robbie tried to clear the route to the doorway while Megan sat on the grass near the building, looking out for approaching cars.

It took time, care and a couple of ropes to ensure James was lifted above the path and out to safety. He was thankful for the fresh breeze that revived him. To his left he could see the helicopter. He had never been in one before and was nervous. His leg was beginning to hurt more intensely and he knew he would have to get to hospital as soon as possible. Megan shouted as a car appeared at the top of the road. Soon the children were joined by their mothers.

Megan's mum rushed from the car first and hugged her. They went over to James and she spoke with the men as he was being taken on board the aircraft. Robbie ran over to Ruth, who had been driving. She got out the car and put her arm around him.

"Are you ok, son?" she asked.

"Yes," said Robbie, but he wasn't sure if he was. He hadn't had time to process what had happened.

"Where's James' dad?" he wondered.

"He was working nearer to Lerwick so he's going straight to the hospital now. James' mum, Alison, is going with him and we are taking Megan home with us to wait for news."

Megan and her mum came over to talk to Ruth briefly.

"They say he should be ok," said Alison with relief. "Are you sure it's ok for you to take Megan? I'll phone you as soon as I can."

"Of course," said Ruth. Megan stepped towards her, reluctantly.

Once Alison was safely on board, the others got into the car to watch the helicopter take off. When the rotors were spinning at speed and the engine noise had increased, it slowly rose off the ground and turned to head south. Ruth allowed the children to watch it disappear from view before starting the car. Megan was unusually quiet.

"Don't worry, love, he's in safe hands now," Ruth tried to reassure her. "You've both had a real fright but you did the right thing and your actions will definitely have helped James. I'm proud of you."

Later that evening the children sat in the living room with hot chocolate and blankets, for comfort rather than warmth. Ruth had made chicken and chips, which had gone some way to cheering both children up as they waited for news. Alison had let them know they had arrived at the hospital safely and that James was going for an x-ray. Robbie put on a DVD; he didn't say much and Ruth knew not to force him.

A couple of hours passed. Alison called again to say James had needed a small operation to realign the bone in his shin before it was put into a plaster cast. The doctors said that it would take at least six weeks to heal and that James would need to use crutches. Ruth spoke to a neighbouring farmer and he agreed to pick up the children's bikes in his trailer. But, despite all the hopeful news, neither child slept well.

The next day the children didn't feel like doing much. They wandered around the shed and watched some television but couldn't muster the enthusiasm for games or the concentration for reading. In the afternoon Megan's dad arrived to pick her up and take her to the hospital to visit her brother. James was recovering well and was relatively free of pain. He was sitting up and talking. Ruth gave Megan some cupcakes to take with her and Robbie watched as the car left their driveway. He looked at the three bikes which had been discretely propped up near the house and he wondered when the children would next be able to use them together. He wondered how responsible he had been for what had happened, how guilty he was.

Over the coming weeks Robbie became a little withdrawn again. Megan was rather impatient with him; what was there for him to be sad about, it was, after all, her brother that had been injured and she was feeling ok now. James was back at school, getting sympathy and attention from his classmates and growing used to his crutches. There were no hard feelings. Accidents happen. But, for Robbie, it had brought back feelings of fear and anxiety. The episode had reminded him how fragile life is, how we are all mortal and how much we take our health for granted. He was distracted and distant.

In his free time Robbie was back in the hills. He often followed small burns to their source up in the peat marsh. He tried to copy and name the wild flowers and plants as they appeared but there were too many for a newly fledged botanist to tackle in one season.

Robbie's collection of small stones also continued to grow; he had gathered many different colours and textures. Some were soft and crumbly, others solid and heavy. Some displayed layers and others shone with glints of silver or gold. Robbie wondered if any contained gems or fossils. He housed them in the empty egg boxes his mother collected for him.

On one occasion Robbie spent an evening filling an old shoe box with earth, moss, pebbles and sticks to create a habitat in which to display a clay bird he had made in an art lesson. He painted the bird to resemble a lapwing and Ruth let him use her clear nail polish as varnish. The smell had been a little overpowering in the shed and Robbie had had to leave the door open for a while afterwards.

A lot of time was spent looking in books and on the Internet for information and ideas. Magnus didn't come over, Megan didn't visit; Robbie's friends seemed to know he didn't care for company. Maybe they had other – more fun – friends to visit, Robbie couldn't be sure. He didn't know how he would feel if they didn't wait for an invitation and just turned up regardless. He didn't know when he would feel better.

"Your dad would be really proud of you," Ruth said quite unexpectedly one day. She had watched her son looking out the window for several minutes. He was obviously lost in thought and over-analysing something intangible. Ruth felt for Robbie and worried about his angst and inner torment. She knew there was little she could do to help him through these emotionally difficult times, except be there.

"Do you think so?" Robbie responded. Ruth smiled and reached for his hand.

"I do," she said. "I really do."

CHAPTER SIXTEEN

Fast food chains, escalators, trains and rivers were not the only things missing in Shetland. Robbie had read that there were many British creatures which could not be found as far north as Unst including foxes, badgers, moles, snakes, toads, bats, lizards and deer. Robbie did not feel he was missing out. He had seen glimpses of killer whales from the ferry, otters from the beach, frogs and hedgehogs in his own garden. The one thing he did miss was trees.

A short walk from the Bed and Breakfast was an old cottage surrounded by vetch, clover and campion. It was empty and abandoned but Robbie could see it would have been beautiful. Set in a small but idyllic garden, it looked out over the bay. But the most compelling thing about the house was that it stood next to Shetland's oldest tree plantation, Halligarth Wood. The trees – mostly sycamore – had been planted in 1845 and were surrounded by a large stone wall. With the help of this perimeter protection, they had survived where almost no others on the island had. While those closest to the sea still appeared stunted, others were remarkably tall and healthy. Robbie had heard that many interesting birds, especially migrants, thankful to find a safe resting place, had been spotted in the area. In spring the woodland floor was a carpet of celandine buttercups and bluebells. At night some locals believed it was haunted. Robbie wanted to see the trees for himself and today was the perfect day.

When confronted with the tall wall Robbie was unsure how to proceed. Luckily, before trying to scale the potential hazard, he discovered the gate, although it was thoroughly rusted and almost ineffective. It seemed a little conventional to sneak in to a place using the gate, but Robbie reminded himself that this wasn't Harrow; there was no need to lock out graffiti artists or vandals here – why risk damage to the wall to keep out a few harmless 'twitchers' and nature-lovers? It was exciting to feel the layers of old fallen leaves under his feet once more. The soil was damp and musty, he could see so many interesting textures; lichen, moss, bark. There were lustrous beetles and red velvet mites dancing in the mulch, and various shapes and sizes of fungi protruding from the darker, damper hollows. The younger trees huddled and struggled under the canopy of the larger mature plants. Their smooth, grey trunks were not yet twisted and scaly. Veiny, leafy hands stretched upwards, grasping for light. Some areas of the wood were scant, allowing nettles to gather their stinging army in huge regiments. Robbie noticed this troop had been in battle with a legion of caterpillars. Beard lichen sprouted all around, its pale blue-green colour clashing with the mustard powder lichen and the bright pink thistle flowers sheltered against the wall.

Robbie carefully meandered through the undergrowth; he counted over two hundred trees. He wondered if he'd be lucky enough to see a raptor, but had to settle for some starlings and a raven. After almost half an hour of investigating, observing and identifying Robbie came to another, smaller, gate. It led to a partitioned section of the wood, overgrown but free of trees. A collection of gravestones stood instead; a private plot where the nature-loving family could enjoy their plantation into eternity. Robbie felt this was not a bad spot to try to rest in peace. Death and life together. He could not seem to enjoy the latter without being reminded of the former. Maybe this was how it had to be. He looked up at the leafy awning watching it sway and triumph over the salty breeze. Time to go.

* * *

Jack hadn't seen much of Robbie for almost a month. He had missed his friend and, while he was not always exuberant, Robbie was both an interested and interesting visitor, so Jack was delighted when the boy made an appearance.

"You've caught the sun," Jack observed. "Where have you been hiding?"

"I've been busy and there's lots to see outside at this time of year."

Robbie told Jack all about the birds, flowers, insects and animals he had seen but the old man knew, despite all this, there was worry inside.

"And what else Robbie? What's on your mind? Something is troubling you. Something has taken that sparkle in your eyes again. Is Ruth ok? Are you missing Harrow?"

Robbie went quiet. He was never sure how Jack seemed to know about the feelings he tried to hide. He wondered how to explain things that he did not quite understand himself.

"Mum's fine. But I've been thinking a lot."

And Robbie told Jack all about James' fall and the blood on his face and the doctors. When the adrenaline of that day had gone, Robbie had been left with flashbacks and nightmares about his dad and falling, shouting and guilt.

"Words like 'fault', 'blame' and 'guilt' are dangerous," said Jack. "They are not helpful. James' fall was an accident. I think his injuries have upset you though, reminding you of your feelings of helplessness when you lost your dad. That would be completely understandable. But I hope you can shake off your negative thinking. You have made great progress since moving to Unst; your enjoyment of nature and your new friendships can help you find your optimism again."

Talking with Jack put things into perspective. There was a lot to be positive about, a lot to fill his time and he needed to keep trying to find the joy in things. But it was easier said than done.

Robbie was tired of thinking too deeply and Jack could see it. He suggested they did a crossword together. Robbie usually read the questions for Jack. Jack always said the answers were on the tip of his tongue and Robbie give him little clues.

Often the answers would remind Jack of an anecdote and he would go off on a tangent, remembering old times and laughing about mishaps and misunderstandings. This was happening with such regularity that it had become a shared joke. After reading each question, Robbie would ask, "Does that remind you of a story Jack…?" with a twinkle in his eye. Jack would reply "Well, actually…" and they'd both laugh. Between them, with some help from passing staff, they managed to successfully complete three crosswords and a wordsearch.

Over a cup of tea and some biscuits, Robbie took the opportunity to ask Jack some more questions.

"Jack, how much money do you think I need to earn when I leave school? And how much money makes somebody rich?"

Jack looked amused. "I think you're maybe asking the wrong person Robbie. I have never been rich. I got by. I had a lot of fun through the years, but most of that didn't cost a bean. I haven't met many rich people who were as happy as I was. They always wanted more and more."

"But I still have to pay for things, like a house and food and bills. How much does that cost?" Robbie asked, with sincere concern.

"You're a bit young to be worrying about that," said Jack. "Keep working hard at school and you'll get paid better when you've finished your education. All the studies will be worth it. Pick a job you really will enjoy, even if you don't earn so much. I think you might like a job in science, but it's up to you. My advice is try not get into debt – just buy things if you have the money saved up, and remember 'things' might not make you happy."

Robbie was not completely convinced that living a life that focussed on 'needs' rather than 'wants' would be much fun. Everywhere he looked on television and on the Internet he saw adverts for a perfect life, physical perfection and materialistic goals. But then, as far as he could see, that bore no relation to the hardworking crofters on the island. No-one walked around with a supermodel partner, no-one drove a Ferrari, no-one cared who designed your cinema room. No-one had a cinema room.

The locals were mostly hard-working, family-oriented, fashion-functional, kind souls who seemed to live a relatively simple but contented life. Little things made them happy. Big things didn't happen often. They were not self-centred or egotistical. They were quite shy and their lives quite routine. Jack was one of them. He had a calmness in his eyes, he had a wisdom and acceptance that Robbie wanted too. He didn't need to go around telling everyone how great he was, he just was. Maybe Jack had money, Robbie didn't know. He liked that he didn't know, because he was ashamed to admit it might have changed things.

"I am thinking of zoology or biology," said Robbie. "Do you think I'll be able to do that?"

"Of course. You can do whatever you put your mind to, if you want it enough. You'll also meet friends who love nature too and you can do outdoor things together."

Robbie decided it was about time he took his current nature-loving friend outdoors and asked if he could borrow a wheelchair for Jack. Once settled, Robbie pushed Jack gently around the cement path to the garden.

For almost an hour the happy pair enjoyed awakening their senses. It was a sheltered spot with a few neat, well-kempt beds and ordered rows of lupins, tulips and primroses. Further back, the garden became an open meadow where several bees explored the wild blooms. Devil's-bit scabious, small orchids and red campion appeared between the sweet vernal grass and yellow rattle. Jack pointed out the white clover and eyebright, all evidence that this was a drier, rather than marshy, terrain.

Tucked comfortably under his tartan blanket, Jack watched the fluttering black and scarlet stripes of a red admiral butterfly flit from one blossom to another. Occasionally, Robbie detected a faint synthetic scent coming from the distant bench that stood next to a 'wet paint' sign.

Further around the path, Robbie parked Jack outside his own room. He fetched a small watering can and filled it from the hose tap. Jack reached up to the window boxes which he had carefully planted a few weeks before. He let his geraniums take a long drink. The moisture released a lemony aroma from the rounded leaves. With gentle care, Jack pulled away some of the dying foliage and flower heads. Robbie took a photo of Jack smiling proudly next to his mini garden and then they both munched on some biscuits.

Towards the horizon, thicker bands of cloud hung motionless over the silvery ocean. Robbie wondered if it would rain later, ensuring the other vegetation would also get watered.

Two curlews flew gracefully across the vista and landed amongst the wild flowers, their long, curved bills poking eagerly between the stems. Robbie looked at their flecked brown plumage and tried to remember what he had read about their behaviour and distinctive call. Shortly, the pair of larger birds were joined by a few shimmering starlings whose feathers appeared almost iridescent, taking on an 'oil-dipped' appearance in the light. Before arriving in Unst, Robbie had always believed starlings were black.

With a little help, Jack got to his feet and took a few steps to the bird table that he enjoyed watching from his room. Taking a small plastic bag from his pocket, Jack sprinkled some seeds and nuts under the sloping, wooden roof. Before he had returned to the wheelchair, one of the starlings was enjoying a lazy feast.

"Well, I'd better go," Robbie concluded. "Tomorrow Alison is taking Megan, James and me to St Ninian's Isle so we can see it for ourselves. James is still on crutches but he's desperate to get out the house."

"I'm in for dialysis tomorrow if you want to pop by and see what happens," said Jack, as Robbie pushed him back around the path.

"I'm not sure Jack. I don't like hospitals much."

"Oh, I understand," said the old man. And Robbie knew that he really did.

CHAPTER SEVENTEEN

With his precious, now dog-eared, nature book clutched in one hand, and a bag of snacks in the other, Robbie got into the car the next morning. Ruth had managed to get help at the Bed and Breakfast and had decided to accompany Robbie to St Ninian's Isle with Alison and her family.

"Are you sure it's ok Mum?" Robbie asked her, "I know you're really busy at this time of year."

"Yes, son, I'm sure. And I'm beginning to think you don't want me to come along," she teased. "Besides, when you told me about Jack, I thought maybe we could see him while James' family is in the hospital to get his leg checked."

Robbie was still unsure but it did seem like a good opportunity to see Jack on dialysis. He had tried to explain the process to Robbie but it was difficult to truly understand what actually happened without seeing it.

The two-car convoy drove the seven miles to the ferry. They passed the turning for Uyeasound and had to slow to a halt for a group of Shetland ponies that had wandered across the road, unaware that there was a ferry timetable to keep to. The first ferry crossing was only seven or eight minutes on a calm day. The children got out and looked over the side into the sea. The metal bow cut through the water creating a V-shaped wake in Bluemill Sound. The children saw a few sea birds and seals, nothing out of the ordinary for Shetland. Robbie had almost come to take these experiences for granted, but he often wondered what his Harrow friends would make of it all.

Robbie noticed how much his perspective had changed. Today the 17 mile trip through Yell was full of exciting glimpses of nature; 'rain-geese' on black lochans and 'peerie-hawks' darting over the cerise-coloured flowering heather. Robbie chuckled to himself.

"What are you laughing at?" asked Ruth, she couldn't see anything funny happening.

"I was just remembering when I was on Skype to Amir in Harrow and told him I was going to Yell. He looked confused because he thought I was going to start shouting at him, remember?"

Ruth laughed too. It was a bit of a strange name for an island. Robbie had researched the island names a little but had found nothing conclusive. He chose to believe that 'Unst' came from the Old Norse meaning 'eagle's nest', whereas 'Yell' came from the Old Norse meaning 'barren' – this seemed to make sense to Robbie, even though he'd never seen an eagle on Unst.

At Ulsta ferry terminal there was a shop and a large area of marked asphalt where cars lined up in lanes. The booked drivers got priority but this was a larger ferry, the Daggri, and an amazing number of cars could fit on it. Ruth had become used to driving onto the ferries but, initially, it had been a bit nerve-racking for her. The ferrymen would coax drivers forward with tiny movements of their weathered fingers and give an abrupt 'halt' sign and a big, friendly grin when the manoeuvre had been completed without a bumper or wing mirror collision. They came around to collect tickets and money, whatever the weather; in winter Ruth had been told the journey could be pretty terrifying.

As the safety announcement was informing passengers where the 'muster stations' were, Megan and Robbie scurried up the stairs into the passenger lounge, leaving James to accompany the adults in the lift. Robbie got a cup of hot chocolate from the machine. They all sat at a table near the large glass window in silent awe. This crossing, through Yell Sound, would take longer; about 20 minutes. Alison and

Ruth chatted. After five minutes James closed his eyes for a mini-snooze, lulled to sleep by the gentle rocking motion of the vessel. Megan and Robbie quietly identified passing creatures.

"Puffin. Another one. Four puffins."

"Guillemot."

"Gannets diving over there." A smudgy finger point on the glass.

"Ummm. Seals. Two. Grey or common? Grey, I think."

"Black headed gull."

"Common gull."

"Arctic tern. And an oystercatcher."

"Not fair, you said two."

"Ok. Arctic tern."

"Oystercatcher."

"Not fair."

"Is."

And then the engines revved and the Daggri started to turn and slow, positioning herself for vehicles to disembark. The ferrymen raised the bow of the boat and waved off the cars, one by one.

🐑🐑🐑

St Ninian's Isle lay south of Shetland's capital, Lerwick. The small island was only actually surrounded if the seas were unusually high. In all other circumstances it remained joined to Mainland Shetland by the largest tombolo in the UK. The tombolo was a 500 metre long strip of beach which, unusually, had the sea on both sides, making it feel like a sandy bridge to the isle.

Megan and Robbie ran across the shingle, racing to St Ninian's Isle, the others following behind. Robbie took some photos to show Magnus. He skimmed stones, paddled a little and then he and Ruth searched for driftwood which was dry enough to burn.

A short while later the group was sitting around a campfire. The delicate flames licked the barnacles on the wood, curling and growing like new shoots searching for the sun. The fire was encircled by stones which provided shelter and safety. In the blaze Robbie could see glints of silver – not treasure, but tinfoil wrapped around half-cooked potatoes. As if about to start a fencing match, James and Megan held kebab skewers out towards the flames. Pierced marshmallows melted in the heat, blackened and sometimes caught fire themselves. Alison and Ruth watched closely and held out chocolate digestives for the toasted marshmallows to land on. Megan passed a biscuit to Robbie.

"Marshmallow, you have been burned at the stake but now you must meet your fate – prepare to enter the jaws of death!" Robbie said dramatically before eating the lot in two mouthfuls. Food definitely tasted better outdoors. And you were allowed to eat your desert before your potatoes.

Out at sea, a small boat bobbed on the waves. A man exercised his collie dog at the other end of the beach, throwing a ball into the shallow water. Megan and Robbie walked up onto St Ninian's Isle.

"What a beautiful place. I can't imagine what it would have been like to find treasure here. Or anywhere, actually. But especially here," Robbie said, out loud.

Megan reminded him of their class talk as Robbie wandered about with his trowel, digging, and then filling in, random little holes. He found nothing, except a sheep's jawbone for his shed collection.

"I'll come back with a metal detector someday," Robbie promised Megan, and himself.

Ruth called them down. The potatoes were ready and, despite a distinct smoky flavour, were delicious with a little butter.

Alison and Ruth looked for shells and spoke about celebrities, other people's kids, the power of the Internet and Unst's upcoming events. James and Robbie had a 'sand creature' building contest which Megan judged. She declared her brother the winner because he'd used seaweed and pebbles to give his model crab some texture.

"Right, it's time to go," Ruth declared as she approached the camping area again. "We've got to get to the hospital in Lerwick before three."

Gilbert Bain Hospital looked quite institutional. While the design was not going to set the architectural world alight, it served the islands well and all the staff seemed helpful and kind.

The kidney department – or 'renal ward' – was on the fourth floor. In it, a specially trained nurse greeted them with a warm smile.

"Ah!" she exclaimed, "You must be Jack's friends. He's been hoping you would make it and wants to show you what we do here."

In the dialysis room, Jack sat on a big chair facing a window and was attached to a machine the size of a fridge. Robbie felt a little queasy.

"Robbie! Ruth! Welcome to my 'home-from-home'," said Jack. "Take a seat, but not that one," he said, pointing to the only other dialysis chair, which was empty.

"Here I am on my haemodialysis machine," he began, with surprising enthusiasm. "I sit like this for five hours, three times a week, as you know. Neither of my kidneys work so this machine slowly takes my blood and cleans all the invisible bad chemicals out of it. That's what kidneys are supposed to do." He looked up and then pointed at a red tube that led into his arm. "This tube is clear but my blood is inside it, going to the machine and then back again into here." He pointed at another tube. Robbie was a mixture of fascinated and repulsed. "You know I can't drink too much – that's because the fluid stays inside me and this makes the machine's job harder. I also have to watch my diet because some foods contain more difficult chemicals. You'd be surprised what I'm not allowed – even some healthy stuff, like bananas. They contain things, like potassium, which are no problem to you but make me feel yucky. When dialysis is finished the nurse disconnects the machine and weighs me to calculate how much fluid the machine has removed. I feel very tired on the journey home to Unst but tomorrow I'll feel better," Jack concluded, before asking if there were any questions.

"Does it hurt?" Robbie asked.

"Not really, you get used to the needles. This machine saves my life, so it's worth it. People with kidney failure can only stop using this machine if they get a kidney transplant. There is another kind of dialysis which people can do at home called CAP dialysis, but I chose this one because I have the time for it and I like the nurses to take care of the whole thing."

Ruth looked concerned. "I wasn't aware you spent such a long time on the machine Jack. With one arm connected to the tubes and lying so still, what can you do to pass the hours? Is there anything I can get for you?"

"Don't worry, my dear," said Jack, "I got some fishing magazines from Magnus's father and I try to do crosswords with help from the nurses. I am also used to my own thoughts and there is a television, if I want it. It's just all part of my routine now."

As Robbie recounted the visit to St Ninian's Isle, the machine suddenly let out a loud beep. The nurse pressed a few buttons and told Jack not to move for the final 20 minutes of dialysis.

"Jack, we'll leave you in peace before we cause any more beeping," Ruth smiled and stood up. "We shall see you very soon."

"I take it you didn't find any treasure?" Jack looked hopefully towards Robbie.

"Only this," said Robbie, and he winked conspiratorially at Jack as he pulled the sheep bone halfway out of his coat pocket.

CHAPTER EIGHTEEN

Unst, like most of the islands in Shetland, was speckled with disused croft houses and the ruins of animal sheds and outbuildings. Robbie's favourite two were in the back garden of the old doctor's house. One was used by a farmer to store his hay. It housed bales from floor-to-ceiling, providing shelter for thick, black beetles and creating a sight which would make Rumplestiltskin twitchy with excitement. Tiny windows threw mysterious shadows onto the stone-built walls and the echo of post-sneeze silence hung in the air. The other old croft was used 'for storage' but really this meant it was a hospice where unwanted items waited in a holding pattern until their inevitable last journey to the skip. Plastic chairs with rusty legs, old chalk boards and picnic sets, driftwood and saucepans, rope and a television deeper than it was wide. A stray bale of hay. A damp, mouldy rug crawling with insects and spiders.

On the other side of the back yard was a walled garden. The owner, Mrs Leask, had given Robbie permission to bird watch in it whenever he wanted. Along with Halligarth Wood, it was one of the few places on the island where trees grew. Around the edge, and just to the height of the wall, was an eclectic mix of sycamore, rowan and willow trees. They were part-hidden by unruly grasses that Mrs Leask was unable to control; she did well to keep a lawn of sorts in the centre of the space but it was as much moss as turf.

To repay her kindness, Robbie had offered to cut the grass to clear the garden space right back to the perimeter tree trunks. Once done, the lawn would be easier to maintain and would, effectively, double in size. It was not a completely altruistic act, Robbie knew the job would reveal interesting wildlife as well as being physically challenging.

Over the course of a few days Robbie used secateurs, branch trimmers, strimmers and mowers to remove the unsightly undergrowth. He carried bundle after bundle of cuttings to the most hidden corner of the garden, released and repainted the picnic table and benches, and refilled a long-forgotten planter and a small pond which was surrounded by a makeshift rockery. Beneath the willows was a small hillock of bluebell bulbs. Fragrant cow parsley carpeted the area under the sycamores. Along the back wall fiery-coloured lilies framed the lawn whilst mint and rhubarb were uncovered near the gate. A fruitless but hopeful blackcurrant bush edged up the wall.

Plied with scones and juice, Robbie worked on to expose the garden's potential beauty. His nails were black with dirt, his fingers cut and arms bruised but this went unnoticed by the boy who rarely stopped in the middle of a job.

A small frog hopped between the docks and hemlock. Robbie transported it nearer to the pond, in the hope that there may be more activity there the following spring. Snails and woodlice revealed themselves under rotting pieces of bark and fallen stones. Robbie carefully tried to rebuild the wall in small sections where it had eroded. Creating a solid and beautiful boundary was an art and novice efforts to patch up vulnerable segments were obvious but appreciated.

In the poppy leaves, Robbie uncovered an unusually low blackbird's nest. Used in previous years it was perfectly formed in a tight circle, protected from the wind and the eyes of predators. Robbie considered taking it for his collection, but it was so surprising and secure in its position that he decided to photograph it instead.

On the outer edge of the south facing wall – which could be seen from the back of Mrs Leask's house – there were two flat rectangular outlines. These were once the foundations of a wooden garage and a potting shed, neither of which survived the gale force winds of a terrible winter some years before. Around the garage foundation was a small wall, two breeze blocks high. After discussing possible plans with Mrs Leask, Robbie used two spare planks to seal the opening in the wall where the garage door had been. Over time he filled the wheelbarrow with earth from unused corners of the land around Mrs Leask's property and used it to turn the old garage foundation into a raised flower bed. He bought some plants at the farmers market and potted them in the mini garden, watering them with the hose which was attached to the outside tap. He watched to see if netting was needed to protect the new shoots from rabbits and birds but the geraniums and pansies were happily ignored by the non-humans.

Mrs Leask was very appreciative of Robbie's efforts. She sometimes joined him for some weeding or pruning but, more often than not, they both ended up talking and watching the starling flocks swoop in to sit on the nearby telephone wires. Occasionally he stayed later, until the midges won the dusk-time war for territory and Robbie was forced back home. Once, when he stayed past twilight, his torch-lit escapades were rewarded by the snuffling and rummaging sight of a hedgehog hunting for slugs and balling up when Robbie got too close. Its shiny nose and eyes reappeared after many minutes of stillness and it disappeared into the garden's one surviving patch of longer grass.

Butterflies and bees skipped from flower to flower on brighter days. Robbie had planted some wild flower seeds around the pond area to secure pollinator visits for future years. Grass-cutting was his favourite job. He loved the initial petrol fumes from the mower as it roared into life followed by the aroma of the lawn when blades cut blades. Robbie would lie on the grass afterwards and almost fall asleep in the intoxicating smell.

Whenever a task was completed, Robbie always felt more relaxed, even if his shoulders ached and he could barely bend to pick up his muddy tools.

Gardening was such a multi-sensory experience. The honeysuckle and rose fragrances perfumed the back wall, as if a glamorous woman had just walked by. The texture of mud and bark and grass clippings kept his fingers alert. All around beauty grew and nature sang.

Robbie was always silently contemplating what he saw – did creatures have feelings, did caterpillars taste the mint leaves like chewing gum, why had he never seen a dead bird, except on a beach or roadside? There were always questions.

When the garden make-over was finished, Robbie took an unused plank of wood and leaned it over the top of the picnic table. He carefully sawed it into seven rectangles, cutting a small arch out of one, using his own little hacksaw. He used wood glue and nails to attach the pieces together. Four pieces formed the walls of a cosy birdhouse, two created a pitched roof and the larger rectangle was the solid base to sit it on. The arched doorway allowed smaller, garden birds into the box. Robbie painted on a couple of windows and some mini roof tiles after attaching the birdhouse to a post. He pushed the post securely into the earth in a sheltered area between two sycamores, put some grass and moss inside and hung a birdfeeder nearby. Robbie was hopeful that the following spring a family of birds would be found inside. He smiled to himself.

The following Saturday, Mrs Leask let Robbie have some friends over to play in her 'huge, manicured' walled garden. Magnus, James and Megan came and together the children enjoyed a game of Frisbee and a moderately successful attempt at kite flying. Mrs Leask brought out bacon rolls and warm chocolate brownies, and Robbie and James cooked a few sausages on a tinfoil barbeque. Megan and Magnus used the same hot charcoal later to heat up the St Ninian's Isle leftover marshmallows which they all ate straight off their sticks. Despite there being a picnic table, the children inevitably ended up sitting, or lying, on the grass.

"Here's to a great day!" said Megan, holding up her paper cup of lemonade.

"Cheers!" said everyone, as if they were at a fancy party with the glamorous woman wearing honeysuckle perfume.

"Eugh," said Robbie, half-choking. "I forgot I'd put some mint leaves into my apple juice!"

"What shall we eat now?" said James, teasingly. "Can I tempt anyone with one of the mushrooms we saw, a foxglove or a lovely salad of rhubarb leaves?"

"Are you trying to kill us?" asked Magnus "You know they're all poisonous."

"What!?" said James, in mock surprise and Robbie threw a wet mint leaf straight at him.

When the 'real' food was all eaten, the children cleared the garden and thanked Mrs Leask. They wandered down to the burn which ran from the peat hills into the Loch of Cliff. The shallow water was stained tea-brown but was so clean that, as it slowly meandered, the riverbed could be seen beneath.

Megan took off her shoes, sat on the bank and let her feet dangle into the cool flow. She lay back, picking and inspecting the buttercups and daisies that grew within arm's reach.

Magnus stood on the road that crossed the burn throwing grasses onto the water and watching to see how long they took to travel to the other side.

James slowly made his way next to his sister, careful not to fall on his almost-healed leg. He watched Robbie paddling. Periodically Robbie would bend over and lift up a handful of shingle which he would study closely before dropping again.

"Do you think there's gold in there?" asked James.

"Maybe," answered Robbie, rather optimistically. "The water has really smoothed all these little stones, they feel so nice. Jack has let me try out his old stone tumbling machine. In a couple more days my serpentine should be ready – it will look polished, I hope. I think that's as close to gold as I'm going to get."

"Isn't this where you found that big piece of broken plate that's in your shed?" asked Magnus.

"Yeah, it was just over there," said Robbie. "I think it's part of a Victorian dining plate, maybe someone came here for a picnic because Mrs Leask's great-great-grandmother wouldn't let them into her walled garden." His imagination was running wild again. Robbie pulled out a few more handfuls of shingle but only found a small white porcelain teacup handle.

The children strolled home in a happy silence which was only broken if one of them pointed out something interesting. Robbie gave his roadside discovery the scientifically-dubious title of Longest Slug in the World.

When he got back to the Bed and Breakfast, Ruth asked Robbie about his day and gave him a letter that had arrived, addressed to 'Master Robert Alderson' – which made him feel like his picture ought to be on a 'Happy Families' playing card. The ink and neatly joined handwriting looked curiously familiar.

The letter read:

Dear Robbie,

Thank you for taking the time to write. I am delighted to hear that my treasured nature book has found a loving home. I fondly remember leafing through those very same pages, trying to identify all the wonderful flowers and creatures I was so fascinated by.

Keep up the good work. I am sure some day you will become a famous ornithologist, botanist or researcher.

With very best wishes to you and to your friend Mr Jack, from fellow nature-lover, Beth.

Robbie couldn't believe that his letter to Ms. Wishart had actually reached her and that she had replied. He was about to read the letter out to his mother when she turned to him and said, "I'm thinking about getting some chickens – what do you think?"

CHAPTER NINETEEN

Jack and Robbie discovered that online there was a surprising amount of information about keeping chickens. Although the domestic chicken turned out to be the world's most common bird – there are around 50 billion – Robbie was only going to be concerned with eight, in particular.

Robbie had already painted a sign for the new chicken coop which read Gallus gallus domesticus – the Latin name for his new pets. Ruth was more interested in the eggs than the birds so, under the Latin, Robbie had added 'Which came first, the chicken or the egg?' As only the hens lay eggs Ruth was not buying a cockerel. This was probably a good thing from a sleep perspective.

Robbie learned that chickens are omnivores, eating both plants and animals, and can only fly short distances – for example, to get into trees, which is where they would roost in the wild. They can live for over six years.

The chicken coop that Ruth had bought was basically a shed with some nesting boxes added on to one end and roosting perches higher up inside it. A small opening let the chickens in and out during the day but was closed each night to keep predators, such as cats or otters, at bay. Robbie put hay in each nesting box and a couple of golf balls which, he'd been told, would encourage the hens to start laying eggs (providing they weren't feeling under par...). A couple of ventilation holes near the roof were covered over with a metal mesh aptly called 'chicken wire'.

A double layer of chicken wire was also used to make the fenced off area around the coop. It was taller than an average fence, but Robbie knew the chickens could sometimes fly over it to explore so it was really to deter predators from getting in. Ruth and Robbie were going to give the birds chicken feed each day by sprinkling it within the fenced area, making it more interesting for the animals to search for it. Robbie was surprised to find out that the hens were not allowed to eat leftovers so he put down a few pieces of wood and stones which he would periodically turn over to reveal insects and sluggy-snacks, as well as having an area of bare soil which Robbie would turn with a spade every few days. He also smashed and ground up some seashells for calcium, which the hens would need to make their eggshells. Finally, there was fresh water inside and outside the coop, it was Robbie's responsibility to check it wasn't frozen or empty and his job to collect any eggs. Ruth and her son were to take turns to clean out the hen house weekly, before the smell became overpowering, and the droppings and old hay would be put on the compost heap.

When the chickens arrived, Robbie tried to take a photo of each one so he could attempt to learn which was which. They all looked so similar. He gave them names and sketched them as fast as he could. They were always moving, looking for food and scratching about. Sometimes they would try to peck each other. Ruth had chosen a hybrid variety of bird, Warren Hens, which had the typical rusty-brown coloured feathers, pale yellowy legs and a red comb and wattle around their faces. They were inquisitive and became quite friendly, always running towards Robbie when he arrived with some food, pecking at his wormy shoelaces and bounding over the clumps of grass if he appeared at their gate.

In the first few weeks Robbie would sometimes just sit near the chicken shed and watch the animals' behaviour; how they would forage, feed and drink. Two seemed to like the patch of dandelion leaves, and another three often scratched around the loose soil.

Every day Robbie checked the nest boxes to see if there were any eggs. He was delighted to find a few hens had started laying after just ten days. Their pink-beige eggs seemed so perfect – how did the yolk get in there? Eaten fresh the eggs were especially delicious and bright in colour.

Magnus, James and Megan often came over to look at the hens too. Sometimes they would make 'chicken assault courses' out of planks of wood and upturned flowerpots to see what the birds would do. They tempted the hens by laying out a trail of chicken feed and howled with laughter if any of the creatures looked like they were remotely following the designated route.

When it was especially windy or wet, the birds were more likely to shelter in the chicken shed. Robbie wondered if they could smell it the same way he could. He was glad his shed was a little more fragrant, to him at least. All the same, on windy, wet days he hid in his shed too.

Recent shed additions included another map of the world on which Robbie had marked the migration patterns of some of the birds he had seen, some chicken feathers from around the coop and a gannet's beak. The latter sat next to his sheep jaw bone. Also, on proud display, were half a dozen smooth, green, polished stones. These were the pieces of serpentine which Robbie had put into Jack's tumbling machine, and he had given Jack two pieces to keep as well.

Robbie couldn't believe how long it had taken to smooth and shine his grape-sized stones. Jack had explained that the stone tumbler imitated the actions of rivers and waves crashing sand and shingle onto rocks over hundreds of years, so to achieve a similar effect in a matter of weeks was actually pretty quick, geologically speaking.

First, Robbie had put the serpentine into a small cylindrical barrel – about the size of a large coffee jar – along with some other rocks which Jack said were hard enough to polish. He almost filled the barrel with water and added some course grit. The barrel was attached to the machine which would spin it around, day and night, for a whole week. Once the week was over Robbie had to tip the water and grit into the garden, wash the stones and the barrel, fill it with clean water and add a slightly finer grit to spin for another seven days. Robbie did this several times, each cycle using a finer grit that Jack had given him in clearly marked little bags. The whole caper was rather noisy so Robbie had run the stone tumbler in the back of the garage so it wouldn't disturb the Bed and Breakfast guests.

When the tumbling was finished, Robbie had resisted the urge to open the barrel, taking it to Jack instead. They had opened it together and it was then that Jack chose the two pieces he wanted, both were very symmetrical; one lighter green, one darker.

"They do look like snake skin," Jack had said "I can see why it's called 'serpentine'."

Robbie sat in his shed and looked at his jade-like gemstones more closely. He had read that serpentine could bring inner peace but Jack had said that if you believed a tin of beans was going to give you inner peace, then it probably could too. Ever the cynic.

'Inner peace': Robbie still hadn't got his head around it. Was it something boring – just a grown-up way of saying 'sit still and be quiet'? Or was it a calmness that made life easier to deal with? He shut his eyes, clenching the stones in both hands. After a few moments he relaxed his fists a little – clenching didn't seem to be conducive with finding inner peace, just cramp. His mind jumped between past and future, settling on his thoughts of the next day. Magnus's dad was going to take the two boys out on his boat for a couple of hours fishing.

Magnus's dad, Brian, arrived at the Bed and Breakfast in his battered Land Rover the next morning. Robbie hadn't slept well. He was excited but there was still a shadow hanging over him and he wasn't sure why. In the darkness of night he had felt sad that his father wasn't able to show him how to fish, angry that he'd died and jealous that Magnus had a dad and was free of the sorrow that burdened Robbie.

Robbie hugged his mother as she reminded him to wear his life-jacket for the umpteenth time. He grabbed his rucksack which was laden with fresh boiled eggs, radishes from Mrs Leask's raised bed and Ruth's lovingly prepared sandwiches. Outside the porch door, Robbie was greeted by a calm, hazy light which helped to disperse the repetitive negativity of night.

At the Baltasound marina, Brian put three fishing rods, a box of fishing tackle and a burgundy coloured bag into his boat, the Mirrie Dancer.

"It's safety first, lads," he said. "Life jackets stay on at all times, I do the steering, and watch where your hook is. Questions?"

Silence.

The three got into the boat, Brian started the outboard motor and they gently headed away from the pier and into open water. They began to bob a little but the movement was soothing, rather than sickening.

Robbie looked across the bay and back to Baltasound. He could see his house, the stony beach near the Post Office, Mrs Leask's house, the shop and bakery. With the backdrop of hills, the clouds moving overhead, the smell of the sea; Robbie would have been happy even without the fishing. In front of the boat was Balta Isle, its familiar silhouette sat on the horizon outside Robbie's bedroom window, but he could now see its beach and cliffs more clearly. It was somewhere he wanted to visit when he got his metal detector. Ruth had promised to get him a basic one for his upcoming birthday. 'Balta Isle Treasure' – that had a certain ring to it, he thought.

Robbie looked over at the circular salmon farm cages nearby. He wondered how many fish were in each cage and how much they were worth. Common and lesser black-backed gulls called overhead, whilst some inquisitive fulmars sat on the water.

Brian showed Magnus and Robbie the basics – putting a fly on each rod and casting them into the sea.

"There's a lot of waiting around when you're fishing but that's when the anticipation builds. Who'll catch something first? What will it be? How big will it be? Will it get away?" Brian laughed, as if remembering past adventures.

Robbie wasn't sure how he'd feel about catching a fish, and being responsible for killing it, but he did eat them. It seemed a bit hypocritical to sit on a moral high-horse when Shetland fishermen put their lives in jeopardy to provide him with his fish supper. Having said that, it wasn't everyone who had the stomach to eat something they had previously seen frolicking around – he knew for sure he couldn't eat any of his mother's hens. He wondered if the salmon farmers ate salmon. Maybe you just got used to the whole idea, he thought. Maybe it was just the same as him eating one of the radishes he'd grown in the raised bed. All this thinking was making Robbie hungry.

The trio began to enjoy their sandwiches as Brian told them about his most successful fishing trip. It was a story that Magnus had clearly heard a thousand times.

"Why's the boat called Mirrie Dancer?" asked Robbie.

"Well, 'Mirrie Dancers' is the Shetland name for the Northern Lights or Aurora Borealis, but when I bought her, she already had the name," Brian explained.

There was a noise from the east. Robbie looked up to see Oscar Charlie, the now familiar coastguard helicopter, flying overhead. He hoped the crew were only on a practise exercise. His eyes followed it as it flew over Balta Isle and turned south. The deep imaginings and memories that the helicopter brought Robbie were suddenly interrupted.

"Robbie! Robbie!" Brian and Magnus cried in unison, "Your rod! Your float has gone under."

The thin end of Robbie's fishing rod curled downwards.

"I'm not sure what to do, can one of you show me?"

Brian grabbed the handle and pulled. As the creature struggled Magnus got the landing net ready. Robbie watched carefully as Brian began to reel in the fish; both fought against each other. When the fish appeared Brian wound it in as quickly as he could and dropped it down into Magnus's net. It wriggled furiously.

"It's a beautiful mackerel." Brian was delighted. "First one of the day – should we give him another chance and put him back in?"

Robbie quickly took a photo of the silver fish as Brian released it from the hook. Its v-shaped tail thrashed, the lines on its back still glistened, wet.

"Yes," said Robbie. "Everything deserves a second chance."

CHAPTER TWENTY

"Do you know why you're here?"

The question could be considered on so many levels, Robbie thought as he lay looking at the ceiling of his bedroom. Here? To make the best of things, to be a better person, to enjoy all life had to offer.

Another year older. Another year wiser? He knew the fog was lifting and that, somehow, it was going to be ok. 'Ok' – maybe not 'great', maybe not always 'fantastic', but ok. Ok was ok. He could hear Ruth pottering around downstairs, getting ready for their long-promised day trip to the very north of the island, to Hermaness Nature Reserve, for his birthday treat.

The road ribboned its way past now familiar lochans and marshes, fields and fences. As they left what few buildings there were behind them, Ruth and Robbie moved silently towards sky and space.

In the small car park, mother and son gathered their supplies, as if they were embarking on a long journey of self-discovery. In truth, the walk would probably only take a few hours, but this would be long enough to recharge their souls back to full strength. The ranger had not been able to guide them so they were on their own.

Ruth left a notice in the car. It stated the walk date and start time, their names, contact details, planned route and time of expected return. Sensible. In Shetland, weather conditions could quickly change from restorative to ruthless. Robbie looked to the wide horizon. He closed his eyes and smelled the ocean, the muddy dampness, the scent of open space.

Ruth and Robbie did not say much initially. This was not a place to be marred by chitchat. Ruth thought it was quiet; silent almost. For Robbie, nature was never still. He could hear the high-pitched cries and squawks, the promise of what was to come.

The beginning of the walk took the pair upwards. In Robbie's mind they were starting a quest to reach the secret 'Bird City', somewhere magical to him, full of unknown sights and sounds. Fingers of bracken reached towards the path, as if trying to hold them back. The breeze began to blow ominously, for this was the same breeze that would carry 'The Gatekeepers'...

Exploring the natural world sometimes felt to Robbie like playing a computer game, entering a fantasy world. In Level 1 he might only face the threat of mud or wet feet, but, higher up the levels, he would have to fight through undergrowth, over chasms or, as today, over shelterless moorland, while under threat.

'The Gatekeepers' were the great skuas, or 'Bonxies'. The 'Pirates of the Seas' – large birds who knew no fear, attacking other birds to steal their food, attacking Homo sapiens to steal their view of Bird City. Or, really, to protect their territory and offspring from the perceived threat humans posed. The attacks would consist of rapid, low dives. There was a real risk of being hit – by beak, feet or something decidedly smellier.

When the Bonxies started to attack, Ruth was most at risk, being taller. She had come prepared though, as the Bonxie attacks at this time of year were pretty legendary, and she didn't want Robbie's birthday trip ruined by injury to body or confidence. As Robbie followed closely behind her, she held up a walking stick and waved it above their heads. The relentless dive-bombing did not stop but was raised to a safer level.

Ruth and Robbie continued over the section of wooden boardwalk which lifted them up from the marshy grasses, protecting the delicate ecosystem full of tiny flowers and mosses. Robbie could now recognise many of these colourful gems amongst the woody brown stems and twisted tufts. With Ruth waving her arms furiously above him, Robbie lay down a few times and took phone-photos of the last remaining blue spring squill, bog bilberries and the blooming, papery sea pinks.

'The Gatekeepers' had tried their best but Ruth and Robbie had successfully made their way to Level 3. They could hear the noise intensify. Slowly they walked in the direction of the sea, carefully edging towards the cliff face. To the right was Muckle Flugga lighthouse, marking the most northerly reaches of the United Kingdom. It was exciting to see it, at long last. White wave crests moved towards the rocky shoreline. An invigorating cool wind brought with it the smell of guano and the cries of the 'Bird City'. Robbie could already recognise many species returning from the sea towards their nests, scrapes and burrows.

Ruth put her arm out protectively, indicating that they were almost at the edge. They both put down their bags and lay on their stomachs, creeping forwards on their elbows. Robbie held his binoculars up, out of the sheep muck. Ruth looked at him and smiled.

After a final deep breath, Robbie looked down, over the edge. Every square centimetre of space was taken, the dark cliff face was transformed into a sheer wall of feather and flight. His senses were overwhelmed, the frenzy of movement and noise mesmerised him.

Fulmars and shags, gannets and gulls, puffins and kittiwakes called and fed and flew. How could so many thousands of birds interact with such speed and precision without collision?

For a couple of hours Robbie watched the huge colony intently as birds arrived with fish and sand-eels while their young called for more.

The predominant species was the gannet, the Shetland solan. He watched their creamy yellow heads and streamlined bodies glide on black-tipped wings, their blue eyes focused and alert. He watched them fold back their wings and drop, like white bullets, into the sea, as though they were a machine engineered for that very purpose. He watched them 'billing' other birds near the nest – a greeting which looked like a fencing match. This was far better than any computer game.

With his 'bins' firmly positioned over his eyes, Robbie tried to teach Ruth some of the Shetland bird names, calling them out as he saw them; peerie maa, skootie alan, muckle scarf, maali, tirrick, tystie and, of course, tammie norie. Ruth laughed. She was happy in her own thoughts and mindfulness. She was in the moment too. For a few short hours she did not consider regrets of the past or fears for the future, she just gazed, as if entranced by dancing flames or an orchestral crescendo.

As Ruth passed Robbie crisps and sandwiches, it felt as though they had joined the nesting birds; the adult was feeding the juvenile. They sat a few metres from the edge and turned out of the wind.

"Do you feel older?" Ruth asked.

"Not really."

"I don't feel any different now to how I did 15 years ago," said Ruth. "I know I've got more responsibility and I know lots of things have happened to me but, inside, I'm still the same 'me' really. It doesn't change. Sometimes I wake up and I don't know how I became this old!"

"Mum, I'm a lot happier here now. Inside, I feel like I'm 'me' again, too. I really hated you for bringing me here at first, I thought it would be boring and I would miss Harrow, but it's not boring. I think whatever is around us, if we work with it and learn about it then it's not boring. I feel more alive here. Before, I thought maybe I'd died when dad died."

"Me too. It will never be the same, son, but he'd have wanted you to be happy with yourself and your life. None of this was our fault – it's just no life, always being angry and regretful. Dad would have been so proud of you for not giving up."

"I think he'd like Jack. Jack gives me an idea of what I want to be like. He reminds me that, even though I think I know stuff, I am really just a kid. And I'm lucky to be a kid because, did you know, when he was my age he was already working? No wonder his body is giving up!"

A gannet, caught on a current of air, rose up to their eye line and hovered there for a few seconds. Its beak like a spearhead, its curved body cutting through the wind with the efficiency of a sports car.

"Robbie, there's something I've wanted to tell you, but I didn't know when the right time would be..."

"Are you dating a man from the walking group?"

"No! No, nothing like that, I'm not seeing anyone. I'm not ready for that. No, it's about your dad."

Robbie waited.

"When your dad died, it was a terrible time and so sudden. I wasn't really thinking straight or caring for you the way I should but I made a decision which I think was the right one."

"Coming here?"

"Coming here, yes, but, before that. Your dad was on the Donor Register. He wanted to give his organs to other people. Just like Jack needs a kidney, you know? Somewhere, out there..." Ruth pointed out to the wide horizon which was lit by shafts of sunlight and greyed by deepening clouds. "Somewhere out there are people who have been saved, and are hopefully having wonderful lives, because I agreed to your dad's own wishes. His heart, lungs, kidneys... lots of him, is still changing lives in a good way."

They were quiet for a while.

Robbie tried to take it all in.

"Somewhere dad's heart is still beating, and his lungs are still breathing?"

"Yes, love."

Robbie started to cry. Ruth held him. They sat like that, on the cliff edge, for some time as waves crashed on the rocks below.

"I'm sorry, Robbie." Ruth whispered.

"Don't be sorry," said Robbie. "I'm happy, I don't know why I'm crying. I am sad for us, but happy for the other families. Do you know them, can we see them?"

"No. It's not really allowed. I couldn't choose who got the organs. I don't know where they went, but I did get a letter saying they had been transplanted successfully, although there was no guarantee of that. Medical advances nowadays are incredible, it's amazing what the doctors can do. Hopefully somewhere, out there, someone, like Jack, does not need to go onto dialysis any more. Knowing Jack will help you understand what that really means."

"Dad didn't die for nothing."

"No. He didn't live for nothing and he didn't die for nothing."

They were quiet again. Ruth watched the sea and wondered if the rain squall in the distance would result in a poignant rainbow appearing. Robbie watched the birds.

"The more I look at nature, the more I have to accept that everything has a life cycle. Everything lives and dies. It's what has to happen."

Ruth knew this was a huge step for Robbie. During his time on Unst he had made friends, old and young. He had become more independent and shaken off the depression brought on by devastation and death. Robbie had found nature and learned the importance of passion and peace.

Ruth put her arm around Robbie as they sat at the cliff edge for a few last moments. Suddenly, he sat upright.

"Mum, look!" he cried, pointing at a smaller bird with a black back and a white, rounded tummy. "It's a baby puffin – a puffling."

"Is it? Why haven't I seen any others today?"

"They are in their nests, underground, maybe in an old rabbit warren. Each puffin pair only lays one egg and so it is extra special to them. The pufflings normally leave the nest at night, when it is safer because they're probably only about six weeks old and can't fly properly yet. This one has just left the darkness of the nest all by himself. If he makes it into the sea, he will not return to land for two or three years."

Robbie and Ruth watched as the fledgling tentatively moved towards the cliff edge. Ruth imagined the fear of the adult birds as they watched helpless, hoping they had done enough to give their one baby a chance at survival. She knew the feeling.

The puffling was buffeted back by the approaching wind. It managed to take a few steps forward and then seemed to stop to consider what lay ahead, like a novice parachutist psyching themselves up for the point of no return.

At that moment, the young puffin leapt from the cliff. Robbie and Ruth watched as it hurtled towards the water. It plummeted down, spinning and turning, trying so hard to find its way. Then, just in time, it managed to stretch out its tiny wings and land safely on the ocean's surface.

And so it was with Robbie's own journey into the light. Ruth had nurtured and guided him but, ultimately, he had to travel through his darkness, and solve his difficulties, in his own way.

Robbie was starting to believe he, too, would survive and leave the dark times behind him. He realised that, through life, few journeys would run smoothly. He could not control everything. Life would always involve some freefall. At times, all of us will feel like we are tumbling.

"It is not the strongest of the species that survives, nor the most intelligent that survives. It is the one that is most adaptable to change."

(Often attributed to Charles Darwin)

TUMBLING

SIMPLIFIED VERSION

The following version of 'Tumbling' condenses each chapter into approximately 300 words. Where possible, these are taken from the list of most common words in English or are phonetically correct vocabulary words.

This version allows readers who have recently started to learn English, or those who face some challenges in literacy, to read the same novel as their friends and classmates.

It can also be used as a reminder of what has happened in each chapter, or as a synopsis for children who have missed a lesson and need to catch up quickly.

It should be noted that this simplified version does not contain all the description, punctuation and character development of the longer version.

CHAPTER ONE

Robbie is at the doctor's office. The doctor is asking how he is feeling. Robbie does not know what to say. He is looking around the room and he feels sad. He does not feel like himself. He is very quiet.

Robbie used to live in a place called Harrow in London. He played with his friends there. Now Robbie feels like there is nothing inside him. He cannot look at the doctor or think what to say so the doctor tells him he can go home.

Robbie leaves the room and finds his mother, Ruth. She is waiting for him and can tell he is not happy. Robbie used to be a little bit bad but now he is just quiet. Robbie does not say very much as they walk home. It is a windy day.

This new place is very different to Harrow. There are not as many houses and the streets are almost empty. This is Unst, at the top of the UK. Ruth got some money four months ago and decided to move. Robbie did not want to move but his mum said they had to. Ruth thought it was for the best.

There are no trees on Unst but Robbie likes to look at the sea. His mum is busy working in their new Bed and Breakfast. There is a bakery, two shops and a sports centre on Unst. People like to meet in the hall and play music, dance and eat together. Unst is a safe place. Only 600 people live there.

At the side of the road, on the walk home from the doctor's, Robbie sees some frog eggs in a puddle. They look like jelly. Ruth and Robbie go home. Most days, Robbie just plays on his computer but today he gets a bucket and goes back to get the frog eggs.

CHAPTER TWO

Robbie was born in Harrow. He grew up there. He used to hang out in the town centre, eating fatty food and playing on his skateboard. Lots of different kinds of people lived in Harrow. Robbie's best place was the park. Lots of people went there to play. He liked the plants and trees. There was a nice smell in the park.

Sometimes Robbie went to the graveyard, next to the park. It made him think that life was short. He looked at the headstones, the dates, the names. His friends came too. They tried to get him to do bad things. Robbie did not want to.

Robbie's dad, Nathan, had lived in Harrow too. One day he was in a car crash. Robbie and his mum went to the hospital. Nathan was very ill. A machine kept him alive for two days but then Nathan died. Robbie's gran came to help look after him. After the funeral, Ruth decided to move to Unst because it was safe. Robbie was very sad.

They left Harrow in their car and drove up to Aberdeen. It took 11 hours. Then they got on a boat for another 14 hours. They slept on the boat and woke up in Shetland. Unst is an island in Shetland. To get to Unst they had to drive again and go on two smaller boats. Robbie thought the boats were the best part of the trip.

When they got to Unst, Robbie saw lots of fields and grass. In the new house he found his room. There was nothing much to do so he looked out the window. He could see clouds. He felt relaxed. The clouds were changing and his life was changing.

CHAPTER THREE

The Bed and Breakfast smells nice, clean and new. Robbie's cream coloured room is quite big. Robbie is going to paint it one day. He looks at the walls and does a lot of thinking. He is trying to understand his new world. He thinks about the past and what might happen next.

It is a cloudy day. Robbie goes for a walk. There is a lot of sky and land. He looks at the colours. He can see a lot of birds but he does not know what kind they are. Robbie will soon grow to like birds a lot and learn about them.

Robbie walks to the beach. He looks around, at the sea, the boats and the houses. It is cold but he is wearing lots of clothes. He lies down on his back. Robbie tries to relax. The sea waves come onto the sand. He almost falls asleep.

When Robbie sits up, he feels a bit better. Near the sea he finds some shells and puts them in his pocket. The sun is going down. Robbie takes some photos on his phone. He is glad that Unst is a safe place.

He is about to go home when he sees a bird near two rocks. It is not well. Robbie thinks it might have a broken wing. He wants to help it. He takes it into his hands. Instead of thinking about himself, Robbie is thinking about the bird.

Back at home Robbie puts the bird into a box. He puts some small holes in the box. The bird is black and white. Robbie has seen this kind of bird before. The bird cannot fly. Robbie wants to make it better.

CHAPTER FOUR

Robbie puts the bird box in the porch. He takes off his muddy boots. He tells his mum about the sick bird because he is very upset about it. Ruth does not know what to do. She asks a man staying at the Bed and Breakfast if he can help. The man knows all about birds.

The man is called Charlie. He is waiting for Ruth to cook his dinner. Like Robbie, he enjoys spending time outside. He knows about animals. Robbie asks Charlie to look at the bird in the box.

Charlie looks at the bird and feels it. He nods. Robbie does not speak. He hopes the bird is not going to die. The man tells Robbie that the bird is an oystercatcher. This kind of bird likes to walk near the sea. Robbie's bird has a broken left wing. Maybe it was hit by a car.

Robbie has to give the bird water and food. The bird likes to eat worms. Tomorrow Charlie will take the bird to his friend, a vet. Robbie can go and visit it.

Charlie tells Robbie how to dig for worms and Robbie goes outside. He makes the ground wet and muddy with a jug of water. Then he jumps up and down in his boots. This makes the worms come up. Soon Robbie sees lots of worms in the grass.

The worms are not too slimy. Robbie looks at them and tries to catch them. He digs. After some time, Robbie has lots of worms in his tub. He feeds the oystercatcher about five worms every hour. In between feeds he looks at bird books with Charlie. It is fun even though they do not talk a lot. The pictures in the books look like they were taken in Shetland.

CHAPTER FIVE

Robbie is tired. In the night he came down to see the bird. In summer the Shetland nights are very light, but Ruth is too busy to make dark curtains. There are a lot of jobs to do and Ruth does not have Robbie's dad to help her. At night Robbie thinks about bad, sad things.

Robbie gets up early and has breakfast. He eats cereal – better than worms! Charlie is getting ready to leave Unst. The radio is on. It is a dull day. Unst has almost no trees so it is hard to tell when the seasons change. The wind blows most days.

Ruth has put all Robbie's shells, stones and crab claws into a bowl in the kitchen. Robbie is looking at them when Charlie comes in. Charlie says the bird is looking a bit stronger.

Charlie says he will take the bird to his vet friend today. Robbie has questions. Charlie answers the questions – one about birds that hunt animals for food, and one about why there are so few trees on Unst. Charlie says there is too much salt (because of the sea), that the soil is not deep enough, that animals eat the baby trees and the wind blows them over. Charlie likes to look at the sea, instead of trees.

Robbie's last question is about one of the stones he has found. Charlie tells him he does not know much about stones, but he is going to visit a man who can give Robbie the answer.

Robbie and Charlie go to a care centre where older people live. They meet with Jack. Jack is the oldest man Robbie has ever spoken to. Jack and Charlie talk and laugh, and then Charlie has to go. He leaves Robbie to talk with Jack about stones.

CHAPTER SIX

Robbie decides to try having a cup of tea with Jack. Jack is not allowed to drink too much tea, which is hard because he loves it. Jack looks at Robbie's green stone and tells him it is serpentine. He tells Robbie it will look very nice if he polishes it in a stone tumbling machine.

Jack tells Robbie that Baltasound village used to be full of fishing boats. Robbie's dad had enjoyed fishing, but he had used a rod. Jack then speaks about a white flower which grows on Unst and nowhere else in the world. Robbie thinks his mum would like to see it.

The old man speaks to the boy about all the things that have changed in the world during his life. He does not seem to like modern things very much. He seems to think life today is quite hard. Robbie enjoys talking with Jack.

They watch the sunlight and clouds that are moving outside the window. After a while they speak about old age and dying. Jack says that he feels each day is special and he feels lucky. Jack tells Robbie he should get to know himself better.

Robbie and Jack agree to meet again the next night. There is going to be a sale in the village hall. The money is going to help fix the church roof. Lots of people will be there. Ruth will go too.

The next evening at 7pm, a lady opens the sale. Robbie buys a book about nature. Jack sits and speaks to people. Robbie sits next to Jack and looks at the book. He looks at the bird bit. They have a drink and some food and then the auction begins. People have to bid to win an item if they want it.

CHAPTER SEVEN

The auction starts with a blanket. Next there are some potatoes, and a doll's house. Ruth buys something. Jack likes a red plant and asks Robbie to put his hand up. He gets it for £11.

After a while there is more cake and then the raffle. Ruth gives her raffle tickets to Robbie so he can check the numbers. He helps Jack with his numbers too. They do not win anything this time, but the doctor does.

When the auction starts again the thing Robbie wants comes up for sale – a pair of binoculars. These will help him to see birds that are far away. Robbie only has £8 left but the bids go up more. He is sad. Someone else gets the binoculars... Jack! The old man pays £12, then gives them to Robbie. Robbie cannot believe it. Jack is very happy to give them to his new, bird-loving friend. After that they are ready to go home.

A few days later a note in the shop says the sale made £1814. Lots of people say hello to Robbie. He always carries his binoculars. Robbie explores around his house. He looks at the pond in the field and he begins to draw things he finds outside. He keeps things in his room and puts labels on them.

Soon Robbie has to begin school. His class is a lot smaller than it was in Harrow. Ruth takes him in the car the first time, but most days he will walk or cycle. When they go in to the school Robbie sees the rooms and the children. There is no uniform. This is new for Robbie. In the office they pick up some forms and meet Miss McIntosh. She takes Robbie around and then to his first class – maths. There are seven children in the class and the teacher, Mr Taylor. The class carries on as if Robbie has always been there.

CHAPTER EIGHT

Robbie begins to visit Jack quite often. Jack shows Robbie how to play cards. Robbie shows Jack his nature book and speaks about what he has seen. Robbie says that school is a bit boring and Jack tells him to keep trying. The old man says that in class you learn not to give up because when you are a grown up you have to do what your boss tells you, even if you don't want to. In school, your teacher is like your boss, says Jack.

Jack tells Robbie that when you find something hard you must do a little bit first and then a little bit more, until it is all done. Jack asks Robbie about a girl in Robbie's class – the one he doesn't like at all! They have a chat and a cup of tea. Jack tells Robbie that his kidneys do not work. Some days Jack needs to go to hospital so the nurses can take 'bad stuff' out of his body.

When Jack is looking at Robbie's book he sees a name in the front. It says Beth M. Wishart in old, blue ink. The young boy tells the old man that they can find out who she is by using the Internet. Jack thinks he is too old to learn about computers. Most people just use them to play games and look at pictures, he says. Robbie tells him to keep trying and not give up!

Robbie shows Jack how to look for Beth on the Internet. They find a news story about her in the book too and this helps them. Together they find out that Beth was born in 1956, liked birds and might have wanted a job in a zoo. Once they have finished, Jack asks if there is anything about him on the Internet and Robbie knows the old man is starting to like computers after all.

CHAPTER NINE

Robbie reads Treasure Island after Jack tells him that the writer had been to Unst. Jack also talks about Hermaness – the cliff home for lots and lots of birds. Ruth says she will take Robbie during the summer. He does some more reading about the sea birds so he will be ready.

For now, Robbie is allowed to go to another northern area; Lambaness. He takes his bike and a picnic. The road is very steep and he goes down it very fast. Robbie begins to look around on foot. He can see bumps in the grass.

During the war, Lambaness was a place where soldiers could look for the enemy. Robbie explores the place. He finds a circlular wall where a big gun would have been. He can see the sea and think about what it would have been like during the war. He can imagine boats coming nearer. Now only sheep are coming closer. He has a snack.

He can see a beach far away. It is empty. The waves have a lot of power. The sky and the sea make Robbie feel small but he feels free too. He feels alive. His cheeks are red as he finds a way to get under the ground.

Robbie goes down into a dark room. He puts on his torch. Now he is out of the wind, it is very quiet. He can hear water: drip, drip, drip. He can see green slime. He feels a bit scared. There are old metal bars, hooks and cupboards. He sees some mushrooms and an old, dead sheep. The torch light hits the skull bone. What is this place?

CHAPTER TEN

Robbie is very scared. He runs out of the dark room, lies on the grass and shuts his eyes. Then Robbie gets on his bike and cycles home, as fast as he can.

When Robbie tells Jack, the old man laughs. Jack says it is good to get a big fright sometimes. Robbie isn't so sure. Robbie feels bad that he had been scared of a dead sheep.

Jack then tells Robbie about the Vikings. They used to live on Shetland a long time ago. Robbie listens as Jack speaks about the fire festival called Up Helly Aa. The men dress up and pull a Viking ship along the streets. They carry fire torches and burn the replica longboat.

Robbie asks Jack if he is scared of dying. Jack says he has had a good life but does not know what to expect next. The two friends then speak about God and what it means to live a good life. Jack has tried to be a good man, to love people and be kind. He does not really pray. The old man thinks that Robbie speaks about death a lot.

Robbie goes home. Life is very different on Unst. It is quiet but he is not bored. He looks at the fields and the animals. He sees a bird – the same as the one he has saved; the one that is going to fly free again soon.

Robbie puts on his computer. The last time it was on he had tried to find out more about Beth Wishart. He decides to write her a letter. He tells her he has her old book and he tries to draw her a cartoon bird. He would never have done this in Harrow.

CHAPTER ELEVEN

Robbie goes to the doctor again. The doctor looks tired. He asks Robbie if he is sleeping well and what colours he has painted his room. Robbie tells the doctor that he has painted it black, white and orange – like the oystercatcher. Ruth is going to let Robbie choose the colours for the rooms in the Bed and Breakfast, they are all going to be the colours of plants and animals.

The doctor asks Robbie about his friends. Robbie speaks about Jack and says that the old man has helped him feel better and talk more. Robbie speaks about Youth Club, where he plays football and eats snacks.

The doctor asks Robbie about his dad – has he told Jack about his dad yet? Robbie has not. He misses his dad. His dad did not leave him, his dad did not want to die. Robbie tells the doctor what happened; all the things he cannot forget, and all the things they will not be able to do now his dad is gone.

He tells the doctor that when it happened, Ruth was so sad that her mum had to come to look after Robbie. No one saw how sad Robbie was getting. He felt very down. After a few weeks Ruth began to plan the move to Unst because she did not want to stay in their old house anymore.

Robbie is slowly starting to feel better on Unst. The locals are helping him, and the birds and animals are helping him. After talking to the doctor, Robbie tells Jack about his dad. He speaks about how he feels different to other kids. He worries a lot, but talking helps and he likes to talk about this dad.

Robbie is beginning to see that lots of people have problems, and that bad things happen to good people.

CHAPTER TWELVE

Robbie likes girls but he does not always understand them. When some girls speak to Robbie he does not know what to say. He wishes he was a bird – they only need bright colours to impress. But he is glad he does not need to sing like they do!

Megan is in Robbie's class. She does not know about birds but Robbie still likes her. Robbie says he could teach her about animals. Megan says maybe.

Robbie keeps flowers and feathers. He takes pictures of animals and sorts shells. At Youth Club Robbie asks his friend Magnus to come for tea one day. Ruth makes nice food and is happy to meet one of her son's new friends.

Robbie and Magnus play computer games and watch TV. Magnus is funny and they speak a lot. His dad has a boat and Magnus tells Robbie he can come fishing with them next time they go.

The boys eat too much beef stew and apple crumble. They cannot move for a while, but then they go for a walk. They throw stones and draw. Magnus tells Robbie that there are Shetland names for all the birds. Robbie wants to know the Shetland words. 'Shalder' is the Shetland name for an oystercatcher. Robbie decides to call his bedroom Shalder because of the colours.

Back at Robbie's house, Robbie shows Magnus the old shed. They take lots of rubbish out of it and begin to clean. They fix the holes and put in a stool and two chairs. They paint and make plans. It is going to be their research workshop.

CHAPTER THIRTEEN

School is better than it had been before. The class is small. Everyone is good. Robbie tries to work harder, just like Jack said. Robbie even likes the food at school! There is a pond and a vegetable plot. Robbie likes to stay busy and now he is sleeping better too.

For one lesson Robbie has to work with Megan. They have to do a class talk about something to do with Shetland. Magnus and Chris have done a talk about fishing – it was very funny and they made masks for it.

Megan says they should tell the class about the St Ninian's Isle Treasure. Robbie has never heard about this before. He asks Megan some questions and she begins to look on the Internet.

During the week, Robbie and Megan work on their talk and Robbie makes some fake treasure out of card and foil. They get nervous.

On the day, the pair tell the class about the boy who found silver treasure in Shetland. It was over 1000 years old, so it is in a museum now. Or is it? Robbie puts his fake treasure on the desk and the class laugh. The teacher, Mrs Boyle, says they have done a very good talk.

After school Robbie takes a spade to the garden to dig for treasure himself. There are lots of wild flowers in bloom. Magnus is still coming to do nature work in the shed. They have plants and a little pond in Magnus's old fish tank. Robbie has found a ram skull and hung it on the wall. It reminds him that he wants to go back to Lambaness again. This time he will not go alone.

CHAPTER FOURTEEN

The weeks pass. Robbie and Megan spend more time together and are often joined by her older brother, James. They go to the stream and the pond and look for rare flowers. They draw pictures and talk in the shed.

One evening the children go to the shoreline. They are deciding what to do at the weekend. Robbie says they should go to Lambaness, if they dare! The children speak about their plan and what food to take. Ruth helps Robbie get ready.

On Saturday morning James and Megan cycle to Robbie's house. The next ride will take about two hours each way. They go past the garage and up the hill. On the other side they go down very fast. The sea is a deep blue. They can see for miles. Robbie can hear lots of birds.

They stop at Norwick beach for a snack. The children sit up on the grass. They watch the gannets diving in to the waves, until it is time for the final part of the trip to Lambaness. It is too steep to cycle so the children push their bikes up the last hill.

At the top the children have another short rest. They look at the blue sky and smell the flowers. James almost falls asleep. They cycle down into Lambaness and start walking around the old, underground buildings.

Megan goes in first. The boys go in too. James goes around a corner, into another room. It is dark. He falls and cries in pain.

Megan asks if James is ok. He says his leg is broken.

Robbie tries to phone for help. There is no signal.

CHAPTER FIFTEEN

Robbie takes control. James answers some questions so Robbie can get help. James is trapped under some wood. Megan speaks to him to keep him calm.

Back up the hill, Robbie gets a signal and calls 999 for help. The lady on the line tells Robbie the coastguard helicopter is flying nearby and can pick up James and take him to hospital. She calls their parents and explains what has happened.

The red and white helicopter comes quickly. Two men jump out. They move the wood that has fallen on to James and look at the hurt boy. Another man arrives with a stretcher. Slowly, James is moved. He has never been in a helicopter before.

Soon Ruth arrives with James and Megan's mum, Alison. Alison goes in the helicopter. James' dad is going to meet him at the hospital. Megan has to stay with Robbie and wait for news.

Back at the Bed and Breakfast, Robbie puts on a DVD and he and Megan eat chicken and chips. Alison calls to say that James will have a small operation and will need to wear a cast on his leg for six weeks. Robbie wonders if he is to blame for the accident.

Robbie becomes sad again. The fall has brought back the feelings he had when his dad died. Robbie goes back into the hills, he wants to be alone. He doesn't know when he will feel better. Maybe James' leg will be fixed before Robbie's feelings.

Ruth tells Robbie that his dad would have been very proud of him. This makes Robbie feel a bit better. It is difficult becoming a grown up.

CHAPTER SIXTEEN

Robbie does miss seeing trees. There are a few in a small wood near to his house. They are only a little taller than the wall around them, but Robbie thinks it is a magical place. He knows lots of unusual birds have been seen in the wood.

Inside he can see lots of leaves on the ground and moss on the trees. There are nettles and thistles. Through another gate is a small family graveyard; life and nature, next to death.

Robbie goes to see Jack. He has not been to visit for more than a month. Jack has missed his young friend. He can see Robbie has been out in the sun. Robbie tells Jack all about the birds, flowers, insects and animals he has seen. Jack can tell that Robbie is upset by something.

Robbie tells his old friend all about James' fall and how it reminded him of his dad and made him have bad dreams. He feels he was to blame. Jack tells him it is not his fault and that he has to start to think about happier things again. It is all getting very serious so they do a puzzle together and Jack tells stories.

When they have tea Robbie asks Jack questions about money and the cost of bills and food. He is worried about becoming a man. Robbie decides he would like to study biology.

Robbie takes Jack around the garden. They look at flowers and bees. They eat a snack, do some watering and feed the birds.

Robbie says he had better go, he is going to St Ninian's Isle tomorrow. Jack is going to be in the hospital for his kidney dialysis. He asks if Robbie wants to visit him but Robbie isn't sure. He doesn't like hospitals.

CHAPTER SEVENTEEN

With his nature book and a bag of snacks Robbie gets into his mum's car. Alison is taking James and Megan too. Ruth wants to see Jack in the kidney ward while James is getting his leg checked at the hospital.

On the first ferry, the children look over the side. They see birds and seals. Robbie's Harrow friends would think this was amazing but, for Robbie, it has become normal. The landscape is much more exciting for him now – full of nature and colour.

The second ferry is bigger and takes longer. Robbie gets a hot chocolate and sits at a table near the window. Alison and Ruth chat. James has a snooze. Megan and Robbie look for birds.

Once off the ferry, the two families drive south to St Ninian's Isle. The small island is joined to the main island by a beach which has sea on both sides. Robbie takes photos to show Magnus. He and Megan run along the sand. The children skim stones and Robbie helps Ruth look for wood for a fire. The children toast marshmallows near the flames.

Megan and Robbie try to find more treasure, but only find a sheep bone. James and Robbie make animals out of sand while the mums have a chat. Then it is time to go to the hospital.

Jack is so happy to see Ruth and Robbie. He is in a big seat, hooked up to a machine. Robbie tells him about St Ninian's Isle. Jack tells his visitors how his machine works and how it cleans his blood. It takes about five hours, three times a week. Robbie can't imagine sitting still for that long. Ruth and Robbie say goodbye to Jack and go to find the others. They all set off for home.

CHAPTER EIGHTEEN

Robbie's neighbour, Mrs Leask, has said that Robbie can watch birds in her walled garden whenever he wants. Some tiny trees grow around the inside of the wall. Mrs Leask finds it hard to cut the grass so Robbie helps her. He tries to cut the lawn and clear under the trees. Robbie enjoys the hard work and thinks he will see a lot of wildlife while he is working outside.

Robbie carries cuttings to a compost heap in one corner of the garden. He cleans and paints the picnic table, and puts a flower in the old planter. Mrs Leask gives Robbie scones and juice and then Robbie gets back to work.

Mrs Leask's wooden garage blew away in a strong wind. Only a small wall of bricks is still there. Robbie fixes this small wall and fills it with soil. He makes it into a flower bed and adds plants from the market. He waters it using the hose.

When the garden is finished, Robbie makes a bird box out of wood. He hopes that some small birds will make a nest inside. Mrs Leask lets him have his friends over for the day. Magnus, James and Megan come over to play and eat. They have a great time and then go for a walk down to the stream.

Robbie paddles in the water, looking for nice stones. They are all very smooth because of the flow over them. Jack has let Robbie use his old stone polisher and Robbie is trying to polish his serpentine. On the way home Robbie sees a very big slug.

Back at the Bed and Breakfast Robbie has a letter. It is from Beth Wishart, the lady who used to own his nature book. She wishes him the best of luck for the future. Ruth asks Robbie if he wants to get some hens.

CHAPTER NINETEEN

Jack and Robbie do some research online and find out how to look after chickens. Robbie paints a sign for the chicken coop. Ruth is going to buy eight hens. They will eat grain, insects and slugs. Robbie puts hay into the nesting boxes.

When the chickens arrive, Robbie takes a photo of each one to learn which is which. Robbie feeds them every day and likes to sit and watch what they are doing.

After ten days, a few of the hens start to lay eggs. They taste good. Magnus, James and Megan come over to look at the hens too. When it is wet, the chickens go into their own shed.

Robbie puts some chicken feathers into his shed with the pieces of serpentine he has polished in Jack's machine. It has taken a long time to polish them, but they look really nice now. He has given Jack two stones as well.

One day, Magnus and his dad, Brian, come to take Robbie fishing. Robbie wishes he could be going fishing with his own dad.

The boat moves out, into the open water of the bay. Brian shows Robbie how to put a fly on to each rod and cast them into the sea. And then they wait.

To pass the time, they eat their sandwiches. Brian tells stories about fishing. A helicopter flies overhead. Robbie begins to think about James' fall when, suddenly, his fishing rod moves.

Brian takes the rod and pulls it into Magnus's landing net. The fish moves around. It is still wet. Robbie takes a photo and then Brian throws it back into the sea.

"Everything deserves a second chance," says Robbie.

CHAPTER TWENTY

Robbie wonders why he is here, alive – to be a better person, to enjoy life? It is his birthday. He feels like things are going to be ok. Ok is good enough. Everything is not always perfect.

Today he and his mum are going to go to the nature park in the north of Unst. They go in the car, taking some food with them.

Robbie pretends he is going to visit a secret bird city. The big Bonxie birds try to stop him from getting to the cliffs. They swoop down and attack. Ruth protects Robbie with a walking stick.

At the cliffs Robbie can see the lighthouse. Over the edge he can see a wall of birds, it is amazing. He sees hundreds of gannets and gulls. He tries to call them by their Shetland names.

Robbie and Ruth have a picnic. Ruth ask Robbie if he feels older, but he doesn't. He says he is starting to feel a lot happier and he is glad Ruth has moved them to Unst.

It is a special time. Ruth puts her arm around Robbie and tells him that when his dad died, his organs were used to save some other people. Robbie is comforted to know that there are people who are alive because of his dad; his dad did not die for nothing. Robbie understands everything has a life cycle.

Suddenly, Robbie sees a baby puffin. He and Ruth watch as it tries to jump off the cliff, and into the sea, for the first time. If it survives, it will not return to land for several years.

It takes a big leap. It falls down the front of the cliff, spinning and twisting. It makes it to the sea. Robbie thinks that the baby puffin is a bit like him. He has survived a difficult time. Life is a journey, and there are times when each of us will feel like we are tumbling.

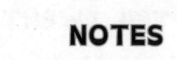

NOTES

ACKNOWLEDGEMENTS

I'm not quite sure how, but this book has taken more than ten years to write. Over that time, many people have kindly supported me and offered their expertise and advice. Thank you to Chris for the inspiration to write the story of Robbie and for acting as unofficial nature advisor. My sister, Kerry, has also been instrumental in putting the final changes in place and ensuring I didn't give up. Thank you to my brother for adding to my happy memories of an idyllic childhood in Shetland and to my parents, Ishbel and Khalid, and to Gran. I have been so lucky in life to have the freedom to roam, the security of coming home to a caring family and to have encouragement for my crazy plans and projects. A group of reliable, intelligent and compassionate female friends have become more and more important to me as I get older. Yvonne dedicated many hours to proof reading 'Tumbling' and found just the right words to pass on her constructive (and accurate!) advice without disheartening me – a beautiful, but rare talent. Gemma, Jenny, Jill, Hazel and Ruth are extraordinary teachers who inspire me in my career, and in life. Thank you to the many wonderful people who have shared paths with me during my travels and at different times. This book is for all those who have shaped the characters I have written about and the experiences I have had; thank you.

ABOUT THE AUTHOR

Kim Karam was born in Pakistan where her mother (from Glasgow) and father (from Pakistan) worked in a Church of Scotland Mission Hospital. The family moved to Scotland and settled on Britain's most northerly island – Unst, Shetland – before Kim was five. After finishing school, Kim studied dance and drama in London for a year before going to University in Edinburgh to complete her MA in Philosophy/Psychology and subsequent teacher training. Kim began her teaching career in 1999 and has taught in Shetland, Edinburgh, London and America, where she won an International Educator of the Year Award. After taking some time out to work in the Scottish Parliament and for BBC Scotland News, Kim returned to teaching and is now a Primary School Head Teacher in Moray.

Kim Karam's first book 'Donation : Transplantation: Conversation' was created as part of her MA in Photojournalism at the University of Westminster. This substantial non-fiction volume was distributed by the Department of Health to patients waiting on the UK transplant list.